HARVEY DUCKMAN PRESENTS...
VOL. 6

*A collection of sci-fi, fantasy,
steampunk and horror short stories*

6e

Published in paperback in 2020 by Sixth Element Publishing

Sixth Element Publishing
Arthur Robinson House
13-14 The Green
Billingham TS23 1EU
Tel: +44 1642 360253
www.6epublishing.net

ISBN 978-1-914170-02-7

British Library Cataloguing in Publication Data. A catalogue record for this book is available from the British Library.

The authors assert the moral right to be identified as the authors of this work.

Printed in Great Britain.

These works are entirely a work of fiction. The names, characters, organisations, places, events and incidents portrayed are either products of the author's imagination or used in a fictitious manner. Any resemblance to actual persons, living or dead, or actual events is purely coincidental.

CONTENTS

FOREWORD

BY JON HARTLESS

When Sixth Element Publishing started the Harvey Duckman Presents… (HDP) in 2019, their intention was to do away with the traditional rules of publishing in favour of a model which benefited the writer as much as the publisher, to draw together the widest range of new writers imaginable, and finally – and perhaps most importantly – they simply wanted to present the best, varied and most quirky examples of horror, scifi, fantasy and steampunk.

In this they have succeeded brilliantly, bringing together a range of voices which have proven to be both diverse and imaginative in tone and setting, from fantasy to horror, hard science to humour, from demonology to steampunk and many points between. New voices and fresh stories proliferate, as per the original intention.

Yet something unexpected also happened. Harvey began to attract published authors whose characters and universes were already formed. Writers who had already constructed their own living, breathing, functioning worlds. Writers who often had no place for these stories to be displayed, for myriad reasons. And these stories often found a home in the HDP series.

The practical upshot of this is that the Harvey Duckman Presents series has become far more than a simple collection of tales. Instead, they have become a gateway to new worlds already in existence, worlds eager and ready for readers to stumble in and explore them. So, welcome to this, the sixth volume of these stories; enter, enjoy, and do explore beyond the confines of the book, for chances are a much wider universe already awaits you, featuring at least some of the characters to be found within these pages.

•

Jon Hartless was born in the 1970s and has spent much of his life in the Midlands and Worcestershire. His latest novels, steampunk motor racing adventures examining the gulf between the rich and the poor, the powerful and the dispossessed, started with Full Throttle in August 2017 and continued with Rise of the Petrol Queen in 2019. The third of the series, Fall of the Petrol Queen, debuted in October 2020.

Find Jon on Twitter @orpingtonpoppy and on Facebook at www.facebook.com/jonhartlessauthor

DISTANCE

ANDY HILL

To me, Seb is just my brother. That he is now some kind of crazy symbol for the future for our crazy Earth still astounds me. His story already seems to be becoming a mythology, yet I know it's true, I was there. But I run ahead of myself. Perhaps we should go back to where it all began.

2120 was much like any other year that I can remember, except for the arrival of my little brother Seb. Mum had struggled with her pregnancy and the midwifdroid's algorithm computed she couldn't have Seb at home. We all knew at the time that transfer to the hospital IsoPods was a big deal. Going outside your touchcluster needs so many approvals and so much preparation. They say a tonne of anti-spread plastic per trip is used up getting in the birthing bubble process. That, like everything doesn't come free. If you can't trade your wares for it now you are dishing out trade notes far and wide. Other than for the first day and the last day of your life, you have to stay with your cluster. You have to. Of course, there are exceptions, the Keys as we call them. Largely they live in one giant cluster and are devoted to mainly making the plastics and a few other specialist things we can't make or grow ourselves. These plastics are important to us as the only way to build the quarantine bridges for intra cluster trade, as well as securing our pods. Our cluster grow salads and market garden, a skill we passed on through generations of perfecting the process against all the odds.

Oh, I didn't say our name, did I? We are Cluster Rocket Leaf, named after the first lettuce we perfected.

Not all the clusters have fared as well as us. So many have struggled to make and trade something the other clusters needed. So many withered away, eventually succumbing to the Soylent Green support plan. They say the idea came from some old film, those people from the old times I guess imagined how we live now, then went out for a steak. One of the saddest things, is staring across our blurry viscose bubbles, to see our fellow cluster neighbours, reduced to trading the proteins of their dead and dying for the meagre essentials. But that's how it is, you just have to get good at what you do and stay good. So many of the clusters end up on Soylent, well it was just too much for them with the deformations. I'm not gonna go on here on what we all have seen, but just so little DNA variety left in each bubble. I saw what happened at the end to our neighbours. They were hydraulic engineers and brilliant at it, for decades they kept our sector hydrated from the springs, and without them we never would have got our greenhouse irrigation system going. Their kids were so weak, so much deformity and weakness, they withered like sunflowers in winter. At least our clusters are safe, I mean who the hell would be crazy enough to mix with another cluster?

So back to Seb. At least we heard he made it safe and well from the birthing pod. Mum was okay but I knew she struggled with claustrophobia. The heat and tightness of all the plastics in those pods. They say it's like the mother is smothered in a hot pulsing cocoon of plastic, as close, hot and visceral as the umbilical confinement of her baby. All that prodding and muffled talk from the medi-cluster people, I knew would be tough. Their scary blurred faces and chatter through double sheets of Visqueen, it made for an unnatural start to nature's most natural event. But it all looked good, Seb was strong and wailing, I was told. I learned later that there was a big worry, as mum and dad were the fifth generation of cousins in my hereditary line. Our cluster was originally just three families, which by now are just as one gene pool. We've been lucky so far in that respect with the outcome.

•

Last year was the big celebration. It was the centenary marking the great 2020 virus war. What's clear is nearly everyone was killed off, what's not clear is what people died from. But we do know when the clusters mix you are doomed. With so few humans left by 2030, it's amazing we are still here now. Since our academic clusters died out from not producing anything useful, we don't know a lot about what happened. So much then was written and spoken onto old electrical plastic and it's all useless now. We know the people kept going into family clusters then coming out in waves. Each time it got worse and people got hungrier. At first there were the key workers and Netflixers (we don't know what that means but they all talked about it being amazing, maybe it was some sort of religion). The key workers went first and the Netflixers emerged when the key workers couldn't supply them. It got ugly in the end. The few of our forefathers and foremothers that made it stayed in their clusters. Gradually and painfully the ones that survived were those that had useful skills to make and grow what they could trade. Go outside your cluster and die, fail to produce usefully and die. We are the rare few that clung on and celebrated 100 years of the precious victory of survival. No one wants to throw away our chance at survival, but perhaps we haven't yet had a chance at life.

•

But then on the way back from the birthing pod, some sort of big accident. It was so far away and we don't know exactly what happened to the auto-pod transfer, but Mum got knocked out it seems and has no memory. Seb was fine but so far away from us that would have been it, if not for the Vaxxers we think who took him. These guys were known as Zealots and nutjobs, they move around outside the clusters, insistent that all of our lives and ways are part of some giant conspiracy. Mum arrived back still unconscious in her beat up sealed pod, via the trade tunnel, Seb's pod was gone. That's what we learned all that time ago, you mix you die, that's it.

It was said the AntiVax lot had been wanting a cluster baby to prove some sort of point, we had no idea what. Once we learned they had Seb, we knew he was lost.

We wouldn't have needed force to get him back but he was infected from another cluster, so he would infect and kill us all. That's if he was even still alive. It's that cruel and harsh but we are survivors, we do what we have to do to survive. Revenge is something we can't afford.

•

2121 changed everything

It was day sixty-two of the year, seeding time. I was out in the cloches. Actually let me wheel back on that, I'll guess you don't have our growing skill? So our home pod is your usual plastic reinforced dome, just like all the others. We live in the hub of the pod, which is also where we process and pack what we grow. The growing however goes on in the cloches. We have three hundred and sixty of them, like spokes on a wheel striking out in all directions. Yep, you guessed it, we work it like a compass, that way everyone quickly knows where all our shit is. The cloches are semi-circular arcs, only a metre or so high and one hundred metres out. We expand each one out at the end of the growing season by another metre, with the plastics we reuse as we trade it for our stuff. Every year we can produce a little more as we expand, the long-term plan being to support our slow growing population and increase our ability to trade.

During seed time, the smaller and younger of us crawl out and plant, checking the watering kit is working okay as we move along. All told, there are six of us fit enough and small enough to hack it. On a good day we get through three cloches each, so we can complete seeding in the twenty day planting window. This stuff is the grunt work, the real big skill job is the seed gathering. No one has our seeds. We could trade them in an instant for pretty much anything with the other pods, but then in a few years our food would be grown everywhere. Those seeds keep us alive. It sounds selfish but then the guys in the nearby pod that make our hydroponic fertiliser ain't gonna show us their secret sauce either. They take a half our crop as trade and we know they sell it on. Without Hydroponic Fertiliser cluster we are finished, our soil was long exhausted, now it's water, sun and the chemicals those guys make for us. But we need them and they need us. Frankly it stinks but it's balance. We could rob and steal from each other but just get infected. That's why we don't have crime, all those crazies killed each other years ago by mixing or fighting in their own pods. The survivors were only us that worked together and traded at distance, but I wouldn't use the word 'fair' to describe it.

Anyhow I digress, I know but you gotta understand this stuff is… well was, a big deal.

•

And there he was, though the murk and glimmer of the cloche walls I saw them. The Vaxxers ambled up towards me. I knew this was bad news. They don't give a rat's ass about the rules. They must have seen me as well, a green and pink blob dragging along the floor of the cloche with my bag of seeds. I had no chance to shout the alarm before they sliced open the top with a knife. I was laid flat out staring up at them. I thought I was fucked.

"He's yours now." That's all they said. Put him down beside me and walked off as calm as Hindu cows.

It had to be Seb, I knew it, there was no doubt. He had the tell-tale extra stuff growing on him most everyone in our cluster is stricken with. I'm not telling you what they are, we hide them and keep it to ourselves. I don't have to tell you everything.

'My brother's back and I am dead.' 'My brother's back and… I… am… dead.' Saying it in my head over and over didn't help. That's it, I'm infected and doomed. If they don't seal the cloche quick all of my cluster will be dead in a few weeks. That's if it's not already too late. Sure, I was a wall of panic and fear but something was odd, something just didn't add up. Then it hit me.

"He can't be alive." I said it out loud, as if to check the words themselves made sense. He should have infected them, they should have infected him. But he lives, my brother, he lives. Maybe I will too?

It wasn't easy dragging us both back down the cloche. All the fumbling and shuffling woke him. He took one cranky eyed look at me and started wailing in all directions. I guess someone in the Vaxxers became known as Mum to him, for sure that ain't me. All the commotion and wailing I guess had set folks in the cluster into a confused panic. Then I heard what I dreaded, the wall breach alarm had been sounded. That triggers the cloche end shutters going down. With the cuts the Vaxxers had made, I was now to all intents and purposes outside anyhow. I was exposed. I was in contact with someone outside the pods. The rules are clear, I'm now an outsider.

•

So I kicked my way out of the crawling tube and sprinted round with Seb to the trading tunnel port. All our pods have a trading tunnel, a cylinder two metres high stretching from pod to pod. Usually there was a simple track and either rope pully or solar motor cart with traded goods. The rule is they sit for seventy-two hours to disinfect. What they disinfect of or from, I have no idea, nor does anyone else. Most of the stuff traded we see isn't for us, it trades across the network of tunnels. That's always been our limitation. Selling fresh, we have four tunnel routes, which in turn connect to four more, so three quarters of our trading pods have to wait six days to get our food. It does a little better when we ship in winter and the tunnels are cooler. I knew I could use the comms cable and cameras there to speak direct to pod control. They would be shitting themselves and thinking only about the end of the pod and a cruel death for all. My best chance was to show Seb and explain to Mum and Dad, they had to be our greatest allies and best chance. It was a slim chance.

I hit the call button and the video screen popped up. They answered with no delay, clearly they had been waiting for this. They were a lot of angry eyes staring back. "What the fuck have you done? You complete idiot," was the first greeting. I can't be angry with them, that's exactly what I would say, if I thought someone had deliberately compromised us all. In the grainy background I saw some haunted eyes as well. It was Mum, she looked lost and bewildered. This was my moment.

"Mum, look, it's Seb. They brought him back. He's okay, I'm okay, it can't be, but it is." I took a pause for breath and to gauge their reactions, just blank incredulous stares. They didn't believe and I don't think I did either to be truthful. "Mum, I don't know why but he's not infected, it didn't happen." Then I said too much. "Maybe the infection ended a long time ago, maybe we've been living this like because we were frightened but now we just like it like this."

Now they weren't looking at me, they were looking at each other. The screen went blank.

In that moment I was no longer the family member, the essential cloche worker but just another outsider, another risk to deal with. But I wasn't just a threat to their health, I was threat to an entire way of life. Staying in the cluster was no longer just a practical response to a biological threat, it was a religion. For those pods that had mastered their trade, this religion was a generous provider. The pods that have survived were those with balance, which usually meant a small group of the strongest calling the shots. You have to understand that meant those pods that put pod before family often fared better. I didn't know how far Mum and Dad would go to protect Seb and I. What went on between them all remains a mystery to me, just a screen of static and hissing for what seemed forever.

Then the screen flipped back into life. It was just Mum, with a gaunt, tormented yet blank look. Events were going in the direction I feared.

"This is worst thing I have ever had to do, son. We have

all talked and it's clear to us, Seb is some sort of terrible mutation, that's the only reason he lives, he's infected you and it will kill us all if we let you in. I can't. I'm sorry. Please forgive me."

This time to screen didn't go to static, it went dead. They cut the power. We are out.

I had only one thing left to look at, Seb. Frankly in all the panic I never really had a proper chance to look at him. I didn't see at first the note left in his blanket wrapping. It simply said, 'If we are right and they won't let you back, come to Hydroponic Fertiliser.'

Honestly I had no idea how, what or why but clearly I was part of some plan. It seemed none of this was an accident.

Moving between the pods is no big deal, if you don't have to use the web of the trading tunnels. By straight line it's less than a mile to the Hydroponic Fertiliser pod, the same journey with our produce takes six days with decontamination twice. When we arrived I was astounded. The Vaxxer guys were waiting by the door as were the Hydroponic workers. I'd always imagined their pods were all test tubes and bubbling bottles but this was much more than that.

"Hi, come over," they said.

"It's all safe, you have nothing to fear," called a tall guy in glasses.

I edged my way nervously toward them. I shouted back, "I might when you tell me what's going on."

And they did. Boy, they did.

•

That was all a month ago. I don't live in a pod anymore. I live in one of these things they call houses, sited just over the horizon, so as not to freak out the other pod people.

It's a lot to take in but it turns out the hydroponic folks did more than make our fertiliser, they were descendants of something called biochemists. They figured out generations ago that the virus had died out. They have been sending out missionaries for years to try to convince the pods that living outside and mixing was possible, but without success. In the end they figured the balance worked best as it is. They supplied us with chemicals and medications, in exchange for the best of what we all made. They did really well taking and trading our food, which they knew they didn't need to disinfect. Oh and yes, they made Soylent Green for the worst of what we make. I never said they were nice people. Maybe life is just a business after all. Now they also have the last piece of the puzzle. Willingly I gave them those seeds in my pocket. The one piece of the biological key they couldn't synthesise. I was cast aside for some crazy religion, but at least the religion of business is open to reason. In a stroke, without killing anyone, they moved a step closer to dominating the human world. And everyone else just let them for fear of change.

Seb and I, we'll miss our families. But we have a way to lettuce remember them by.

•

Andy did one thing for most of his life, then decided to do nothing. Nothing quickly turned out to be everything and now he's too busy even to talk to himself.

He also writes poetry, which can only be read with a Plutonium milkshake.

He is normal. Are you?

FIREFLIES

J.A. WOOD

Moonlight glinted off a razor-edged sickle in the reeds, as the barge pulled close to the riverbanks.

"You watching, boy?" came the grainy voice of Delphine, behind me.

I gritted my teeth, and turned away from the murky window, to find her in the gloom. The Harvest Land's oldest survivor was watching me from beneath her tattered hood. She was crouched on the far side of the mouldy shack, with a hand pressed to the door.

A hashed together pistol swung from her belt. Delphine called it the last resort. Sometimes I wondered what the point of it was since the creatures out there didn't seem to notice when a bullet went in them, let alone die.

"I'm watching," I said, trying to keep the agitation out of my voice.

"Good, because you gotta tell me the second they make their move, or we're dead."

"I know. You tell me every time."

Delphine cast scathing eyes at me, lifting what would've been an eyebrow, except now it was a scar. Most of her face was. "I promised I'd get you to the Syphon, didn't I?

That means you listen to me. Fifty years I've searched for it. I didn't need to bring you along at all."

"Well I paid enough for it," I muttered.

"It was a paltry amount, Gero. You begged me to take you with me. So if you really want out of the Harvest Lands, you keep your mouth shut and listen."

"That's all I've done since we…"

Sloshing water made me look back through the window. The barge came to a stop on the banks, and a makeshift ramp dropped into the foul-smelling mud. One of the crew whistled for the passengers to disembark. That was a big mistake, I thought, even if it did work in our favour.

The glint of metal caught my eye again, making me tremble. I forced myself not to shout out a warning, remembering we'd been holed up in this festering shack for almost a week now, living off the floorboard grubs, stale bread and rancid water. We needed bait to get out, and it'd just turned up.

"Anything?" Delphine asked as she shuffled around behind me.

I held up a hand and fixed my eyes forward, trying not to lose control of my bladder, as the passengers crept along the banks. You've already been spotted, I thought, trying not to wretch at the guilt chewing my insides.

Panic spread through the passengers when from out of the ferns, lurched the Harvesters. Their hunched forms were bundled up in brown robes, clagged with blood and grime. Beneath their straggly hair, were faces hidden under a mess of bulging veins that crawled into their mouths like centipedes. Each wore a makeshift basket on their backs, filled with the spoils of a recent harvest.

My skin itched with sweat as they circled their prey. Silver reflected off the brown water, as the blades came down, crashing against the ribcages of those unfortunate enough to get caught.

Screams ripped apart the silence.

The stench of blood, mixed with the stagnant river, drifted in through the broken glass. More harvesters materialised from the reeds, cracking their victim's ribcages open like shells. Blue light escaped into the air. Fireflies, they called them, the only true light besides the moon, in the darkness of the harvest lands, and we all had it inside of us.

One man tried to scramble away, but he was cut down and his chest was opened up. His killer had a wicker basket-come-bucket on its back to capture the fireflies, and I always wondered why the Reapers never gave them the same equipment.

Then again, no one really knew who the reapers were, just that they ruled this land, and wanted the light. I smoothed a hand over my chest.

Everyone wanted the light.

Escaped fireflies drifted into the air. There were so many. Most of them got away. All this slaughter for a few fireflies hardly seemed worth the carnage, but I watched, almost paralysed as metal scraped and tugged at flesh and bone.

The Harvesters' dull eyes started to focus on the

blue lights. "Now," I cried. "They're chasing the light." When I turned, the door was open. Delphine was already gone.

Two-faced bitch! My body jerked forward, and I went tumbling out of the shack. Tepid mud splashed around me, and the air was filled with screams. Scrambling to my feet, I tore into the darkness, scissoring my hands wildly into the sticky ferns. Water sprayed when I paused and turned to check behind me. Fireflies twinkled in the sky, and the screams were starting to die down. The Harvesters were nearly done with them, and here I was, out in the open.

I crashed through the ferns. Blood pounded in my ears, as the swish, swish of sickles drew closer, and then I plunged. Filthy water exploded into my mouth, and the blackness engulfed me. My lungs started to burn. I must've been under for almost a minute. When something grabbed my neck, I screamed, letting the dirge crawl down my throat. Smashing through the surface, I lashed out, kicking, spitting out the shit at the back of my throat, before drawing in a desperate breath.

"Shut up," someone hissed in my ear.

Slumping into the arms of Delphine, I took an uneasy breath. "You came back."

She clamped a hand over my mouth. "Only to shut you up. Your splashing is going to draw them to me, you stupid little fuck." The admission cut deep. Delphine had been threatening to leave me for weeks, but I didn't think she'd actually do it. Dingy water was stinging my eyes, and my chest burned, but the anger shot enough adrenaline into my muscles for me to jerk away from her.

"I gave you every coin I had, and you were just going to let me die."

"What do you expect, boy? You're holding me back. You can barely look after yourself. This is the closest I've ever been to getting killed by those things, and it's all because of you." She kicked water at me. "It's also the closest I've ever been to the Syphon, and I'm worried you're going to…" She straightened up, poised like a fox at the sound of a dog barking.

"What is it?"

She pushed a bony finger to her lips. Heavy panting could be heard through the reeds. Delphine yanked me into the water, leaving only our heads above the surface. At first it went quiet again. Until there was a soft rustling, and water droplets plinked against the brown leaves, bobbing on the swamp. Delphine pointed to a gap in the ferns where broken timbers floated away from a dilapidated cabin.

One of the passengers stood alone amongst the debris, eyes burning with fear. A shadow fell across him, and he looked up before letting out a small whimper. Leathery, elongated, fingers stroked his head, before curling around it. The man fell to his knees, repeating a mantra too quietly for me to understand. The sudden smell of piss made my nose sting.

The Harvester drew the sickle close to his neck. Weird. I'd never seen them do that before. They always went straight for the fireflies, while their victims were still alive. Frantic splashing tore through the air as another Harvester approached. The first one flinched, took the sickle away from the man's neck and powered it through his ribs.

The scream bounced like a stone off the water, enticing the other Harvester in. The odd gentleness that had overcome the first one was swept away in a battle between the two. The second Harvester wrenched the man from the other's grip, and threw him to the ground, mercilessly driving the sickle through his ribs, before the first tried to reclaim its prey.

My skin went cold, 'cos in that moment I caught the man's gaze. He stared at me, blood spilling from his mouth, and I just watched him. Sickle blow after sickle blow, fireflies sprayed out, too fast for the brawling harvesters to even collect. In the end, after they'd near torn him apart, they probably caught about six for their trouble.

"They'll chase the ones floating nearest to the water for a while," said Delphine. "We need to go now."

"Why didn't we go sooner?" I almost cried. "We could've got away." I hated her in that moment. She'd made me watch it. I was sure of it. Like she needed someone else to see what she had all these years.

"Run? When two Harvesters are in the madness like that?" She let go of my waist, discarding me the way the harvesters did of their victims.

Pulling myself out of the water, I shook out my ragged

jacket and trousers, before following her. I should've just walked away. The longer I spent with this wretch, the more I understood how she'd survived all this time. Plain selfishness, using whoever she could as meat shields to escape. My body weighed a ton with fatigue, yet my mind was frantic, full of hell and rage.

But after an hour of walking, it started to fade. The rage settled back into fear, and the fear made me follow her like a lost soul. I looked up at the cloaked woman in front of me, and the white hair flapping about on her head, like tufts of filthy cotton. She tossed up her hood like she'd heard my thoughts, and hunched over against the hot wind. If she was so bad, she would've thrown me to those two harvesters back there. I let out a lingering sigh and jogged up to her. Something else occurred to me.

"Why did they fight over him?"

She snapped her head up, her face one big snarl beneath the hood. "What are you prattling about now, Gero?"

At least she didn't call me boy this time. "The two Harvesters… Why did they fight each other? Don't they all serve the Reapers?"

She tutted like I'd asked the stupidest question in the world, and then stopped to peer over the sandy ledge we'd traipsed up to. "Stories tell that the Reapers reward those who bring them the most fireflies." Shrugging, she sniffed loudly before hugging her cloak around her, despite the humid air. "Though I don't see what kind of reward you could possibly get in this land. I just want to get out of it."

Without another word, she took off, walking dangerously close to the edge. For a moment I thought she was going to stride right off it, like the Harvest Lands had finally beaten her.

"Who are the Reapers?"

"How should I know?" she snapped. "They probably don't even exist."

"They have to exist," I said, pulling down my hood.

"Why would you want them to?"

The question made me stop. Delphine swore under her breath, grasped my wrist and started tugging me along.

"Because they need to exist. There has to be someone doing this," I trailed off and peered into the dark lands, lit only by the sickly moonlight, and lanterns from distant settlements.

She let out a ragged laugh. "If you say so, boy."

We didn't talk after that.

Delphine found us a place to rest in a squat, fungus-smelling cave. I took a bite of the mouldy bread she begrudgingly gave me, as she dumped herself by the weak fire, prodding a stick into the tiny embers.

"How far is the Syphon?"

She tutted. "I knew there was a reason I never had kids."

I laughed softly. That wasn't the reason. No one really wanted kids out in the Harvest Lands, but sometimes they just happened.

"We're close now," Delphine said, after a few moments had passed. She stabbed the embers again, making the flames spit, and release a chalky odour. "But I'm going alone."

Startled, I looked up at her, and tried to form words. All she could do was wipe her nose on the back of her hand, giving me a flat stare. Then she rummaged into her soaked clothes and pulled out a purse, before chucking it at me.

"There's your money," she said, and then looked away from me to glare at the flames.

"But I…"

"The closer we get to the Syphon, the more harvesters there'll be. I can't risk dying because of you. Feel free to look for it on your own, but you ain't tagging along with me."

The purse slipped from my fingers, chinking onto the floor. "You can't just leave me here."

But she ignored me, and then huddled down beside the fire. White anger blazed in my mind. There was a heavy rock beside my foot. Slowly, I bent to retrieve it.

"Don't bother, Gero."

My fingers grasped the rock tightly, but after a few moments I let it drop, because the thought of being alone in the harvest lands any longer than I was about to be, extinguished the fury. I sank to the cave floor beside the fire and tried to sleep.

•

I couldn't remember a time when I didn't wake up in the darkness. Sometimes I wasn't sure if I ever had. My back ached from lying on a cluster of stones, and the cave was freezing since the fire had gone out. The darkness was too thick to see, but when I padded my hand where Delphine had been sleeping, the spot was vacant. She'd abandoned me.

Something scratched in the darkness. The air turned sour, and the cave seemed smaller. Carefully, I lowered my hands to the ground, ready to push up and bolt, but somehow the darkness ahead of me was thicker than normal. Cast over a silhouette, was a pale sliver of moonlight that moved from side to side. My legs trembled as I reached across the cave floor. My hand touched a rock. I snatched it up and hurled it at the silhouette.

A dull thud echoed into the cave, and the shadow lurched forward.

"You little idiot." Delphine jumped out of the shadows, waving the pistol in the air. "Why didn't you stay still?"

I stopped listening to her though when the Harvester reached me. Hot piss leaked down my leg when leathery fingers gripped my shirt. There was the whoosh of a sickle. I kicked out and threw punches that landed helplessly into squishy flesh. Then fiery pain erupted in my chest.

The thing loomed over me, its mouth inches away. I jammed my fingers into its eyes and we tumbled to the floor. Crawling from beneath its bulk, I tore out of the cave. Blood dripped from a deep cut in my chest, and beneath the skin I could see the blue lights, throbbing inside like a thousand heartbeats.

A hoarse scream came from behind me. I skidded to a halt, spun back around and watched Delphine fleeing from the cave. Moonlight sparkled against the blood dripping down her side, and she was limping. For a moment I just stood there, trying to stop the fear from overwhelming me, my mind ticking over with memories of our journey here.

Delphine had left me alone.

I started running, but then stopped again.

She'd come back for me.

"Run, you idiot!" she yelled, but I couldn't just leave her.

From out of the cave, charged the Harvester. I sprinted back to her, but it got there first, and slammed her into the ground. She let out a rattling scream, but before it could sink the blade into her ribs, I shoulder-barged the creature, sprawling us both to the floor. Shuffling back onto my elbows, I kicked out, frantic and breathless as it clawed its way over to me.

A loud bang clapped the air, and fire lit the sky. The harvester flew backwards, and I hauled in a breath. When I looked up, Delphine was clutching the pistol. Wisps of blue smoke slithered out of the muzzle, and the air was thick with the stench of charred metal. She dragged me off the ground and shoved me into a run. Scuffling feet sounded from behind us. Then a sickle tore my jacket. I shrugged it free and bolted.

Delphine stopped, twisted round and squeezed off two shots.

"Come on, Delphine!"

She ignored me as the bullets thumped into spongy flesh. Twice its knees almost buckled, but it managed to retain its balance, lumbered back up and continued the chase. Delphine planted her feet in the ground. I ran back to her, tugging on her wrist to go, but she shrugged me off.

"Damn it, Gero, run."

For some reason I didn't. I just clung to her arm like a cobweb, and watched as the harvester trudged towards us. Delphine growled under her breath then closed an eye, before raising the pistol. She squeezed the trigger. This time the bullet sank into the canister at its back. A wheezing sound shrieked out of it then moments later, a stream of blue fireflies followed.

The harvester ground to a halt. It must've been the first time I'd ever heard sound coming from one. It wasn't a scream. It was a suffocated groan. The creature shrugged the canister from its back, and tried to plug the hole with sinewy fingers, but the sky was already filling with luminous blue light.

"Move, now." Delphine broke into a run.

I couldn't move though. The harvester peered inside its canister. A muffled groan escaped from behind the cluster of veins at its mouth. Wrenching its finger from the hole, it tipped the canister and plunged its hand inside. The frantic rummaging seemed to last an age, and I stood there, watching its desperate search.

Then it stopped. Its face contorted, and the groan deepened. Slowly, it lifted its hand out, bringing with it a single firefly. Inside its balled fist was the tell-tale blue light, flickering like a rapid heartbeat through the gaps in its fingers.

"What are you doing?" Delphine clipped me across the head.

The fear returned, along with the blistering pain in my chest, making me slink away. I limped after her but glanced back one last time as the harvester fell to its knees, clutching the firefly.

•

The blood had slowed to a trickle, but it was still leaking out of my chest all the same. The grogginess wouldn't seem to pass, and Delphine's incessant chuntering wasn't helping much either. I peered at the cut on her leg, and then at the one on her side, realising just how close it had been for us both, though at least her wounds had stopped bleeding.

"You came back for me," I said, softly.

"Idiot boy," she said, though there wasn't the same venom as usual.

Beyond the stepped plateaus, a grand structure poked out of the horizon, only visible by the flurry of blue light shimmering around the metallic fortress, and the soft moonlight blanketing the arid land.

"The Syphon?"

"I think so." Absently, she gripped my waist and helped me along. Another hour of trekking through dead grasses, and abandoned shacks went by before we reached it. The metallic giant towered some hundred feet over us. Unruly vines and thorns twisted around its base like veins bursting through skin, and birds' nests almost covered a faded façade.

Delphine forced the rusted door open, startling the birds into the air. Their disharmonised cawing made me jump, reigniting the pain in my chest. It was still bleeding and sweat covered my body despite how cold I was.

In the doorway, Delphine paused and then turned to face me. Her eyes went straight to the wound. "Hurry up, Gero, before you freeze out here." It was the kindest she'd ever spoken to me, and that was terrifying. I glanced down at my chest, flinching at the blood saturating my shirt and the tiny strips of blue light poking through it. Forcing myself to look away and ignoring the strange taste of metal on my tongue, I followed her inside. The reek of chemicals and animal shit made me wretch, further aggravating the wound.

Delphine's breath clouded in the air when she let out a heavy gasp. I could just make her out, scouting frantically round a vast altar room, lit by strange green flames. Her actions sent a spike of sadness through me. She was almost rabid. This woman had been searching for a way out of the harvest lands for decades.

One night months ago, in a dingy stop off bunker, bundled away in a corner from the other pilgrims,

Delphine had drunkenly let it slip to me about the old maps she'd finally discovered. There was a way out, a way to escape the Harvesters. I'd begged her to bring me here, and so many times she'd tried to get rid of me. But I was here at last.

The legendary Syphon.

All we had to do was release the fireflies.

The metal building was like one huge silo. Lining the walls were glass tubes filled with thousands of fireflies. It was the most beautiful thing I'd ever seen. I let my eyes fall to the centre, where a stone altar rested beneath a glass disc, suspended by two chains.

"That has to be them," Delphine said, her voice shaking a little. She was pointing at some double doors, at the back of the Syphon. "The way out of the harvest lands."

I nodded slowly but found myself peering at the altar again. "And this is the way to open it, like you said?"

She spun on her heels, cloak twirling like a tail around her. Her eyes narrowed and she walked hesitantly over to the strange mechanism. "I guess it is," she muttered, smoothing a hand over the block. When she did so, the glass began to hum. Delphine snatched her hand away as though she'd scalded it.

"Will it work?"

She shrugged, looking a little fearful. It was the first time I'd seen such an expression on the formidable woman's face. "I have no idea, Gero," she said, quietly. "So it's told in the legends." Delphine straightened up, as though to recite an epic poem. "It's the toll out of this place. Once the extraction's complete, you're no use to the Reapers anymore. The doors will open."

After that we didn't speak for a while, just stared at the ancient-looking thing. If anyone had found it before, and left the harvest lands, it must've been some time ago.

When my eyes started to blur, and the pain in my chest burned again, I looked up at Delphine, wincing, and then smirked. "Go on then. You've been searching for this thing longer than anyone. After you."

She looked up, and frowned, but then humoured me with a smile. Tentatively, Delphine patted the block, stroking it as she lowered herself down. The glass disc started to hum, and then filled with iridescent light. I'd never seen light like that before. The humming grew louder. I took a step back, watching as thin beams trickled down onto Delphine's form. After a few seconds the lights moved back up, and my heart fluttered at the sight of fireflies dancing out of her chest. She was crying, but a euphoric smile accompanied the tears.

A low creak echoed from behind me. I jerked around to look at the double doors. Dust puffed out from the cracks, and the walls shuddered. Then tiny splinters of light escaped into the room, making me yelp and turn back to the altar.

"It's working!"

A rare laugh came from Delphine, as she weaved her fingers around the escaping fireflies. I watched as they were absorbed into the glass, like rain being sucked back into the clouds. Then the fireflies were gone and the light retreated into the disc. Delphine stretched to her feet, shaking a little. "What did it feel like?" I asked, clutching her arm to steady her. "Did it hurt?"

She swatted me away, though not unkindly. A rueful smile appeared on her lips. "A strange feeling of emptiness, my boy, but a price worth paying, if it means freedom from the reapers."

"They're still closed though."

Delphine nodded sagely at the altar.

Cursing my own stupidity, I let go of her arm and shuffled towards it. Everything was starting to disappear around me, hidden behind the black dots marring my vision. Blood fell across the altar as I hauled myself onto it, and there was a rattle in my chest, one that wasn't being caused by the fireflies. I laid back and peered expectantly at the disc, but it remained still. "Is it broke?"

Delphine's upside down face appeared above my eyes. "I'm afraid not, Gero," she said, and something about her tone drove a shard of ice through me. I began to move but she slammed my head back down, and kicked something on the base of the altar. Seconds later, my arms and legs were being clamped down. When she finally let go of my head, I craned my neck up to see the tarnished restraints coiled around my wrists and ankles.

"Delphine, what's happening?"

The restraints pulled taut as I thrashed against them.

"I'm sorry, Gero," she said, backing away a little, and I was certain the doors creaked again. "Truly I am. But I did tell you the reapers reward those who bring them the most fireflies. They promised me they'd let me leave the harvest lands."

"No, I saw the fireflies being extracted from you," I cried. "The door's already opened. We'll be able to leave soon."

"I'm sorry," she said again. "That was just a projection, and the doors don't open to let people out. It's to let them in. I tried, so many times to be rid of you. I gave you countless times to discard me." She sighed, and scrubbed a hand across her face. "I always try to get them to hate me, but they never do. Not until I bring them here, anyway."

"How many fireflies do you have to collect?" I screamed, making her flinch away. "How many people have you brought here?"

"Too many, too many." Delphine turned away from me after that. I heard her repeat the mantra even as she left the silo room. Even as she left me alone, staring up at the disc. I thrashed against the bindings, fear surging inside me when it started to hum, and green veins spread throughout the glass. Somewhere, beneath my own mad cries, I heard the doors again. This time the silo was flooded by red light, and when I turned to face the doors, they'd been peeled open. Eight robed figures floated out, forming a circle around me.

They each looked up, and within their brown hoods, I could see two blue pin pricks staring at me.

"Delphine! Come back, please!"

But she never did. I hauled in a breath, ready to scream

again, but the green veins on the disc began to puddle above my head, and a sharp, beam of light shot down. I closed my mouth but the needling light tore through my lips, and crawled down my throat. The scream never surfaced. It was ripped away with my fireflies. Helplessly, I watched the blue spores being sucked right out of my open mouth, absorbed into the disc. My insides squirmed and my muscles ached, and I lay there paralysed as the final firefly was extracted.

My head thumped back on the slab when the light vanished. The Reapers had their hands outstretched, coaxing in the legions of fireflies. Not once did I think there would be so much light inside me. Now there was none…

My lips were raw and swollen, and everything felt dry. I could barely smell, the air tasted like blood and my skin was sensitive to touch. I tried to speak but only a raspy groan came out. Slumping back on the altar, I tried to breathe, tried to find the fireflies inside of me. But they were all gone, and I was still here. I was still in the Harvest Lands. Except now the light was truly gone, and I wanted nothing more than to feel it again.

One of the Reapers loomed over me. It said nothing. Instead, it gripped me beneath the arms, lifted me from the altar and hauled me like a corpse outside, back into the darkness, back into the harvest lands. For a moment I just lay there, trying to speak, but only the same dry groan came out. Delphine had vanished, and so had my fireflies.

Staggering to my feet, I peered half delirious around

the dark landscape before daring to look down at my hands. Fear drove its way through me when I saw the leathery skin. Only a muffled groan came out when I tried to scream. My throat was like sand, and my skin like a dead pig's.

Dingy moonlight bounced off the puddles, caught within the gaps between the broken flagstones. There was a voice deep in the back of my mind, begging me not to look. I did anyway. I hauled my dead-weight body to the water and lurched over it.

Everything fell away. Staring back up at me was the face of a Harvester. I stared back at it for what seemed like hours, before slamming a fist into it repeatedly, trying to scream through my parchment throat. The wound on my chest was gone. Using my elongated hands, I tried to find it and tear it open again. But it was healed. If only it would come back. Then my blood would leak away and I could go with it, out of these lands.

The darkness swirled around me, and then a cloud seeped into my thoughts.

Fireflies.

All I wanted were fireflies.

Picking my way through the litter at the base of the Syphon, I salvaged a rotten bucket, and shards of scrap metal I could use as a blade. Then I went out into the endless night to harvest.

•

J.A. Wood lives in the North of England with her fiancé and daughter. She has been writing for as long as she can remember, using it as a way to make sense of the world around her. Failing that, she decided to create a new world in her head, populated it with imaginary friends, and spends her free time obsessively writing about them. And in between looking after a feral toddler, and publishing her first book, she also writes short stories that fall within the realms of fantasy and horror. Her debut novel Tethers, the first of her Scorched Chimera series, is due out in 2021.

THE TOWER

MARK HAYES

You never notice the tower at Southbridge when you first see the town.

You never noticed the tower at all, most of the time. It has a way about it. A way that allows it to slip out of sight behind nothing in particular, even when you're looking straight at it. For reasons that are hard to explain, when you're looking at it your eyes would inevitably be drawn to something else. Mundane things would strike you as far more interesting than the tower ever could be. Not that it would be something you'd think about. You never really thought about the tower at all which was, I suspect, the point.

Travellers, that rarest of commodities passing through town, would often find themselves bemused should the tower be mentioned by a local in passing. Much as the locals would be equally bemused if a traveller asked about the tower. Generally, they would assume such inquiries were about the inn in Market Square. This was, it must be said, not an unfair assumption. The inn was after all called 'The Tower' and had a neatly crafted, painted sign for the benefit of those who couldn't read, hanging on hinges that squealed as it blew back and forth in even the lightest of breezes. This occasionally wrong assumption was seldom pointed out by anyone. After all, someone mentioning 'the tower in the market square', was likely as not referencing the inn, not the two-hundred-foot-high, slender, wand-like tower that dwarfed every other building in the town and had an evening shadow which should've fallen across the whole square.

Well, at least, it would've done if the tower actually cast a shadow, but as the local explanation goes 'it chooses not to'.

The locals of course knew the tower was there. It'd be impossible to live in the non-shadow of a building so spectacular and be unaware of its existence, no matter how unobtrusive the tower chose to be. But the thing is, when you see something every day, which does everything it can to encourage you to ignore it, you learn to ignore it.

Besides, "It's just there. It ain't like it makes a habit of moving about or anything," Rudolf the baker's lad told me once while we were taking an eighth day's afternoon laze by the fountain across the square from the tower. A ritual young men of the town engaged in every eighth day in the hope that one of the young women of the town might join them. Which is something I can tell you from sad experience seldom happened, as the young women tended to gather by the other fountain across the square in the hopes, the wisdom of years has taught me, that one of the young men of the town might join them. Such has been the dance of courtship in Southbridge for generations, neither side willing to meet the other halfway. Though in fairness halfway between those fountains is the tower.

Now it must be said that Rudolf the baker's lad wasn't a deep thinker. In the scheme of things he was a lad perfectly endowed in the brains department for rising early, kneading the dough, thinking about the lass who worked in the taproom of The Tower Inn, and trying to guess the likelihood of her coming by the fountain that afternoon. If, however, you wanted to discuss comparative philosophy, he wasn't really the lad for you. So, his observations on the tower were little more than regurgitated local wisdom. The kind of wisdom common to most of the good burghers of the town. Much the same as if he'd looked up at a red sky one evening and told me, "There will be rain on the morrow." But that said he was right enough. The tower, well… it was just there.

You see, the tower had been a fixture in Southbridge and had been for longer than anyone could remember, and if pushed they'd probably tell you it had been there longer than their long dead grandfathers could remember. It was 'just there' and had been 'just there' for a long, long time. This in no way explained a damn thing about it to my mind, but then in fairness I wasn't a local, and as the collective wisdom of the townsfolk would have it, you have to humour people who seemed a little over impressed by a two hundred foot tower of gleaming white stone, that somehow managed to be unobtrusive in spite of itself. They explained such interest in 'the tower' by that other piece of oft spouted Southbridgian wisdom "Outlanders… they be a bit strange in the head."

To give the locals their due, they'd seldom say such a thing in front of an Outlander. It was, however, exactly what they would say behind your back and whether you were in hearing range or not. Just so long as they weren't looking you in the face at the time.

It may seem strange to you that I was considered an outlander, born and raised, as I was, within half a day's walk of the town. But Southbridgian's are an insular lot, and to their mind to qualify as a local you had to be born within the non-shadow of the tower. This was an unspoken but nevertheless important rule in the collective consciousness of the townsfolk. While if pressed they wouldn't admit it, a man could move into town within a few days of his birth. He could be raised there, educated there, work an honest job, meet his soulmate, marry, father children, grow old, die and indeed be buried on cemetery hill. But the good folk of Southbridge would still chisel into his tombstone, 'Here lies John Dodd, a nice bloke for an Outlander, but he'd some funny ideas'.

So Outlander I was, though I'd been coming to Southbridge since I was nothing but 'a blooming hindrance' according to my Dar. I'd ride into town perched on the back of Dar's wagon when I was sent along with him because Mar didn't want me under her feet all day. Of course, in those days coming to town was a great adventure for the youngster I was and I would tell him earnestly, "I'll be helpful, Dar. I'll help you unload, and, and, I'll not get in the way or anything, honest I won't…" And my Dar would grumble and complain for the look of the thing, but tip me a wink, smile and tell me later he liked company on the long wagon ride.

Along the way Dar would tell me long stories that seemed to have little point but made me laugh anyway. It wasn't that his stories were funny, it was more the way he floundered about in the telling of them, the way he kept losing his thread. He wasn't a great teller of tales my Dar, but he told them with all the gusto and enthusiasm that only a father can have for a tale told to his son.

On those long trips the wagon would plod along the occasionally passable road of hard packed earth, with the very occasional stretch of cobbles laid for a few yards. Once, the road was paved and cobbles merely formed the under layer. But that was hundreds of years past in the days of the old empire. Like so many things left over from the old empire, the road was on its last legs, the paving stones long since 'borrowed' for one building project or other by enterprising vandals. Yet even without the top stones, old empire roads remained better than others if you wanted to get from one place to another. Not that anyone went much of anywhere. The old empire had built things to last, even if lasting meant clinging on by its fingernails to the edge of a roof.

The road ran along the bottom edge of the forest that grew wild and ragged beyond the farms of my family and our neighbours. In the other direction it went to Provincia, the old provincial capital back when the empire was still a thing. According to Dar, it was now a collection of aging ruins with a small village nailed round it, or perhaps he said 'to it'. Though I'm sure he'd never been there himself. It was a good thirty miles away after all. Aside the odd tinker and the occasional travelling troop of entertainers who showed up from time to time, no one much came down that road these days. In theory Southbridge and farms like ours around it were all part of some duchy or other, but as whomever the duke may be no one sent any tax collectors our way, which no one seemed much inclined to mind. A few miles past the end of my father's land the road turned south proper away from the forest edge and cut through the gentle hills before it came down into the northern slope of the valley where Southbridge nestled along the banks of the river.

As you would expect, for a boy raised on a small country farm, my first sight of a town the size of Southbridge came as a shock. I'd have been five or six at the time, and had never been further than my mother's yell from the farmhouse, though in fairness my mother could yell a long way. Up till then, the most people I'd ever seen at one time was during harvest when my dad would bring in a few labourers, or when a troop of gypsies passed our land, which was more often than not the same time. Southbridge was a thriving metropolis in comparison, all the more so on market day. But it wasn't all the people, or the plethora of buildings built on top of each other that took my breath away. It was the sheer noise, the smell and the constant activity. From the hill side the town looked like an upturned ants' nest, stretching either side of the white stone bridge from which it got its name. The bridge was another relic of the old empire, but in better repair than the road because even the dimmest procurer of stone thinks twice about taking down the sides of a bridge. The whole place was too big, too busy, too full of life, noise and smells that would turn a cow's second stomach.

I loved it instantly. Show me a child who wouldn't.

I remember that first visit to Southbridge vividly. Sitting on my Dar's cart like a little prince riding a carriage into town. Looking down from on high at all the interesting and strange people milling around. Then watching Dar discuss the prices for his crop, the cost of his tac and other supplies, with the dozen or so stall holders around the market square, talking a language that seemed foreign to my ears as he haggled over the price of three yards of cloth and some needles for my Mar. Then he came back to the cart with a paper bag full of magic he called 'toffee' he had procured for me from a sweet stall. I remember trying to help him load a barrel of wheat beer at the end of an hour of trading with this stall or that and being roundly told to go sit back on the cart. I even remember sulking for a while, before I remembered the magic bag of 'toffee' and cheering up profoundly as I slipped some more of that magic into my mouth. The whole visit lasted no more than a couple of hours. Even with time for Dar to share a tankard of beer with another farmer or two outside the Inn. Then we were packed and heading back over the bridge and home. Those couple of hours seeming to stretch on forever, yet pass in moments. In the way such things do to a child.

As we headed up the hill and Southbridge slowly faded behind us, my Dar turned to me, playfully jabbed me in my ribs and asked me the question he'd doubtless been dying to ask.

"So, did you notice it?"

"Notice what?" I returned, puzzled by his question.

"The tower in the market square," he replied, winking at me.

"Was that the name of the inn?" I asked. A vague recollection of a sign with a picture faded by too many years in the sun came to mind.

Dar laughed, smiled at me, and continue to laugh for a minute or so as he guided the cart further up the hill. Eventually he drew it to a halt on the cusp, turning it slightly to the side of the road so we were looking back down the valley. Then he pointed down at the town and directed my vision to the middle, where the market lay.

"That tower!" he said pointing out what was suddenly the most obvious building in Southbridge. And for a moment, just a moment, I saw it plainly. The great rising circular tower that dominated the town that lay in the shadow it neglected to cast and raised up towards the havens…

I was young, so I never asked Dar how come he could always see it so plainly, when the tower hid from the perceptions of others. Thinking back now, I've come to suspect it was something to do with him looking with the eyes of a child, the ones he kept in a small leather bag around his neck. But some mysteries are never solved…

For those of you who have travelled a little further afield than a six year old farmer's son, a little perspective on where Southbridge is may help you to get a clearer picture of the town. Though I appreciate travelling a half day's cart ride from your home does count as both adventurous and worldliness in some quarters no matter your age. But to those who spread their fettle a little further afield, and who concern themselves with a world of kingdoms and empires, a bit more information may prove to be enlightening.

The town of Southbridge is on the southern bank of the river Taine in what in the days of the old empire was the Comorian province. One of the last great provinces of the old empire created before it fell into decline. To the north lay the ruins of the old provincial capital of Comoria. Which as you may have noticed earlier was not very imaginatively named. This may have been an early harbinger of the decline of the old empire. When you run out of murderous butchers, or as the old empire called them glorious heroic generals, to name cities after your civilisation is starting down the slippery slope of decline. I will admit this is not the most eloquent of theories, but I believe when you start struggling to find new murderous butchers to lead your armies, someone else will undoubtedly find their own gloriously heroic leaders, or as the empire would have called them murderous barbarian butchers, and start chipping away at the shining light of civilisation, or the tyrannous oppressors, depending on your point of view.

This is all ancient history of course, the old empire long ago declined to nothing more than a few cities with lots of history, vague feelings of superiority, and little else. Most people would be hard pressed to point out the empire on a map. Which is a shame since the best maps were of course still made in the empire. Possibly because when you used to own most of the world, you get very good at drawing pictures of it. At any rate it is over five hundred leagues from what remains of the empire to the old Comorian province, and most people living in Comoria would struggle to find the province on those same maps. Not for lack of intellectual prowess, I should mention, but simply because Comoria was now a collection of small kingdoms and large dukedoms.

A word of explanation may be in order about the difference between a large dukedom and a small kingdom. A small kingdom is made up of several very small dukedoms. Whereas a large dukedom is one where the Duke is powerful enough not to bother with all that tiresome paying homage to kings and rules the land himself. Some large dukedoms are larger than small kingdoms, and most dukes of large dukedoms spend much of their time contemplating how to get the rulers of small kingdoms to accept them as king of their own realm rather than just mere dukes, despite the clear disparity in power between a large dukedom and a small kingdom.

Often this involves convincing a small kingdom by means of war, usurping, beheading of small kings and taking of their thrones. Which generally leads to the small dukes of the small kingdom scattering from those kingdom and trying to do some usurping of their own. Meanwhile the kings of small kingdoms look down their noses at mere dukes of large dukedoms and try to become larger kingdoms by means of marriage, patronage and alliance forging. All of which is just another form of warfare, particularly the marriage part. Though it has to be said, most kings are just as happy to use the more direct form of warfare, particularly if they don't like the look of the prospective bride.

Wars happen. Rulers change. Kingdoms rise and fall.

Meanwhile most border towns change hands every generation or so, after the seemingly obligatory rape and pillaging. Then settle down to pay taxes to the new lord of the realm. Wiser would-be kings try to restrict the rape and pillaging to a minimum in order to avoid too much upheaval and get on with the import matter of taxation, which is another form of pillaging but more organised, and the profits flow directly to the king's purse rather than getting distributed among the rabble.

Southbridge, as you might guess, is such a border town. It borders the young kingdom of Sitifia, which has existed for longer than anyone can remember. The Grand duchy of Nordland, which is not particularly grand in size but has a duke whose ego is considerable. And the kingdom of Frank. Frank is currently ruled by King Frank the

Third, whose grandfather liked his people to remember who is in charge, so took the unusual step of renaming the kingdom after himself. The third King Frank is, like his father before him, a traditionalist, at least when it comes to the matter of the naming of kings, so decided to name each of his children Frank with a view to keeping the dynasty going. This, so I've been told, is somewhat to the distress of Princess Frank, the current heir apparent.

Exactly which of these three realms currently has Southbridge under its banner is doubtless a matter of heated debate between those rulers. Debate that has occasionally threatened to move to a more direct form of diplomacy via sharp bits of metal. Southbridgians themselves, however, seldom if ever express any opinion on the matter and consider themselves to be independent of all three, while remaining perfectly happy with the status quo regarding the town's status. This in part is because the current state of affairs means none of the three kingdoms send tax collectors to Southbridge for fear of antagonising the others.

Now, all this may strike you as an odd state of affairs. If it doesn't, perhaps it should… But what perhaps should strike you as even odder, and I say this in plain view of my own hindsight, is that I, a mere farmer's son, happens to know all of this. Perhaps it would help if I tell you that Political History, Structures and Relative Comparisons of Feudal Economic Structures, is considered an obligatory class in the old schoolhouse in Southbridge. That along with English, Maths and Thermodynamics.

As I say, I say this in hindsight. It never struck me, or indeed any of my classmates as odd at the time. It was just the stuff they made us learn…

Before my school days, trips to Southbridge were a rare thing. My Dar may have liked the company but my Mar liked chores getting done more and Dar could only take one of us along each time. Being the youngest of four, three sons and a daughter, and Dar only going to town once a month or so, made such trips a rare thing. Besides which, if Dar needed a hand with lifting stuff he would take my oldest brother Dan, whom Dar wanted to 'learn the farm' which meant, among other things, knowing the knack of buying and selling at market. It also meant learning how best to chew sticks of straw and the correct way to lean on gateposts. Things my brother Dan excelled at.

Sometimes if he had Dan busy around the farm, which I always assumed meant there was a gatepost that needed propping up for a few hours, Dar would take Jeb for the heavy lifting. Jeb was good at lifting, as long as you told him what to lift and where to put it, in a steady slow voice. Jeb got his head banged as a baby, or so my Mar claimed. So Jeb was, as she put it, 'solid but slow' or as my Dar was more inclined to say 'thick and idle', but his heart was generally in the right place. Slightly left of centre, behind his rib cage.

My sister, Patty, only went to town if Mar was going, which was generally about once a year. Most of the time she helped Mar around the house, and with the chickens.

49

Beasts which require an inaudible amount of work considering they generally just scratch around the yard and squawk at you if you come too close. Patty, it seemed to me, spent most of her time dreaming of a handsome prince coming along to save her from the drudgery of it all. At least that was until she got a little older and started to think more in terms of a solid farmer's son with land to come in to. Handsome princes being something of a premium thereabouts, while you couldn't move for slow witted farmers' sons, with fair looks, a few dozen cows, and a working knowledge of haystacks. By the time those farm boys started looking at her appraisingly, she had already appraised them all and knew their value down to the last sheep. She was nothing if not pragmatic, my dear sister.

All this conspired so that while I was young I got to ride into town once or twice a year at most when Dar needed company more than help. Thus due to its rarity, the sublime magic called toffee and wondrous wide-eyed staring at everything, didn't wane for several years. I did however slowly get used to the sights and sounds of the town. Though I never got used to the weird way in which the tower could slip from your mind even when you were staring right at it. It must have been four years after that first trip, as we rode back towards the farm after a long day's haggling, that I realised I'd never actually asked my Dar anything about the tower. For all the constant spill of questions when we rode to and from town. The tower, both singular in its inconspicuous presence and its imposing domination of the town, had never caused a single question to come from my ever-inquiring now nine year old mind. Not in four long years.

This struck me as rather odd. Which in fairness many things seemed to strike me. But all of a sudden a dozen questions sprang instantly to my lips and spilled over each other in a garbled nonsensical outpouring of verbiage as we looked back at town from the hill as we always did.

My Dar laughed. Then told me to slow down and start over with my 'incessant questionings'.

Several deep breaths later, as I tried to decide which of all my questions was the most important, I could feel them all slipping from my grasp. As if something was forcing me to forget them, even forget I was curious about the tower in the first place. With all the reserves of willpower a nine-year-old can muster I forced myself to remember at least one question, while holding my breath until I thought I'd turn blue, in order to get it out from between my lips.

Then carefully, slowly and pronouncing every word as exactly as I could, I asked him the most burning question I could hold on to. "Dar, who lives in the tower?"

My Dar smiled at me and turned to look back at tower again. Then, while holding the pouch around his neck, he smiled at me and joked, "I'm guessing you're not referring to Old Harry and his wife down at the Inn in Market Square?"

I gave him my best annoyed stare, while feeling somehow strained as if the question, even now it had been asked, was still trying to slip away from me. The pressure to just drop the question and forget it had even occurred to me was almost overpowering. I forced myself to breathe deeply once more and just nodded in reply.

Dar grinned, though I can remember seeing his hand clutching even tighter at the pouch round his neck as he spoke once more, and seemed to visibly wince. "Then if you mean the other tower. The tower. Well then, that would be the wizard who lives there, son. The damnable wizard of Southbridge."

I remember wanting to ask him more, but the day was getting on and we still had far to go. Besides which, questions kept slipping from my mind. Even remembering him telling me about the wizard seemed a hard fact to grasp hold of. I had to force myself to remember what he had told me. I even made up a little rhyme to keep the thought in my head.

> *The wizard lives in the tower*
> *In the tower the wizard lives*
> *The wizard lives in the tower*
> *I know 'cause my Dar said…*

I'd sing that to myself for hours on end sometimes. I didn't know why, though I have the strangest memory of Dar telling me the rhyme himself and making me sing it to him on the road back to the farm that day. Dar was strange like that when it came to the tower, unlike anyone else he seemed to think it was important for me to know things about it. Yet I gave it little thought at the time, nor did I think about that strange pouch he wore around his neck. The one with the eyes of a child in it, as he always told us. Though I never looked to see if that was really the case or not, not for many years, not until I understood a lot more about the world and the tower, and by then I was looking for something else.

It was two years later, after harvest, because harvest always came first, that I was packed off to Mrs Broccoli's boarding house for children, in order to begin my schooling. In those two years I doubt the tower occurred to me all that often. Though I would find myself singing that little rhyme to myself at the strangest times. The stream of questions I'd had that day never reoccurred to me. Thinking back now I would guess on some level I chose to avoid thinking about the tower just to avoid that feeling of being forced not to. I suspect that in this I was far from alone. I further suspect that is part of the trick to it all. The tower doesn't like you thinking about it so makes itself hard to think about, and eventually you just get used to not doing so. Though I think Dar was always the exception to that rule. He only didn't think about the tower because he chose not to, not because it made him do so. Not that I understood why that was the case back then.

School was a strange new world. School and town life in general. I wasn't the only country boy to find himself packed off with two changes of clothes and a bag full of pencils after harvest that year. Indeed, the influx of 'sheep prodders' as the town kids called us, was an annual event. So that first week I not only left home for the first time, to take up residence in a room full of beds and the stink of the unfamiliar, but I also joined my first gang. This too was part of a tradition in Southbridge. The prodders vs the bridges, a war that had been fought for generations with sly trips, digs in the back and scattered books.

It didn't help that us 'prodders' started our schooling two years after the townies. Nor that we did so in stints of six weeks at a time between harvest and sowing, while the townies attended school three days a week all year round. We started behind and were always rushing to keep up. Though I found applied logic, the theorems of dead Greeks, and composite chemistry, easy in comparison to most of my fellows, I still found myself behind the curve of townie education for the first year or so. Yet in time I found myself at the head of the class more often than not, a position, in the strange society that is a classroom, which brings its own problems. Being the smartest kid in the class and a 'prodder' to boot made me unpopular with both the 'townies' and my fellow farm boys alike. But I was the youngest of four and had grown up avoiding the disapproval, fists and feet of my siblings. As such I was equipped to deal with the results of my unpopularity and even though I was small for my age I'd worked on the farm for long enough to develop the kind of stockiness that lends itself well to the odd brawl when necessary. After a couple of fights with bigger boys who were unwise enough to judge strength by height alone, a truce was soon declared, followed by de'taunt and finally acceptance.

It was in my second year, as the last few days of second harvest dwindled, that the headmaster of the school came to my father's farm and took my parents off to one side. Dar, as I remember, looked less than happy about this, yet at the same time he'd an odd look of resignation about him. I didn't know at the time but I'd been marked out by the headmaster as 'a lad to watch' whatever that meant. As such he had come to suggest to my parents I attend school full time and move into town to live at the school itself.

I remember the argument that ensued. My Dar, whom I had seldom heard raise his voice before, was adamant that this was not going to happen. Mar was proud and kept saying 'maybe it for the best'. But Dar just argued back that 'no kid of his was going to end up in that damn tower!' Which made no sense as that wasn't what was being suggested but aside the raised voices I could hear nothing more that was said in that room. In the end the schoolmaster left looking disgruntled and no more was said about the prospect of me going to school full time.

Seasons turned, as they are wont to do, and not much happened.

Not much ever happened in Southbridge. Indeed, if the history I was taught at school was anything to go by, nothing ever happened in Southbridge. While we learned about the rise and fall of civilisations, war and political upheavals, these were all events of the distant past, in distant places. Southbridge existed in its own little bubble it seemed to me. A distant outpost of the old empire that even the old empire failed to recall. The town and the surrounding hamlets and farms, just plodded along in its isolated remote way.

'Forgotten about, or perhaps just slipping from the mind of the world beyond the forest and the distant hills that surrounded the region, almost like the tower in the centre of the town slipped from the mind of those who lived there.'

I wrote that in an essay for humanities, three years or so after that first visit to the farm by my headmaster. At the time it seemed an obvious insight. Yet it caused such a ruckus when I handed in that paper.

'Old Kemp' was a retired miller who spent most summer afternoons nursing a pint outside the Tower Inn on the philosophical benches with the other retired men of the town. In winter they would retreat to the warmth of the tap room and do much the same. But twice a week he taught humanities in the schoolhouse and droned on to a bored classroom in much the same way as he droned on to his friends at the pub, though with less actual interest in his subject matter.

Many of our teachers were like 'Old Kemp', retired tradesmen and women who did a few hours at the schoolhouse imparting knowledge to the next generation of Southbridgians. Schooling is, it strikes me, the art of distilling old knowledge to young minds. The schoolhouse in Southbridge did this in the most literal way. Most of our textbooks were older than our teachers, or our teachers'

teachers come to that. 'Old Kemp' was in some ways the worst of them, as he could make any subject seem dry and dusty with age. Indeed, I only ever saw him excited by anything once and that was when I made mention of that tower in that essay.

I was held back after class and made to wait while the headmaster was summoned. An occurrence that did not sit well with me. I was due to meet Rudolf and the others at the fountain and we were certain, despite all previous evidence, that a couple of girls from the other fountain were going to come over and talk to us this time. In fairness we were certain this stupendous event would occur most every day, yet it always failed to materialise, but as I sat in the empty class room, regretting ever writing that damn essay, I was entirely certain that this would be that sainted afternoon the girls would finally wander over. The one afternoon in the last three weeks I wasn't going to be by the fountain with the other lads.

In short, I was cursing my foul luck.

The headmaster read my paper, then he read it again, fixed me with the kind of stare that make any school kid feel an urge to vomit when you're getting it from the headmaster. Then he nodded to 'Old Kemp' who nodded sagely in return, stood up and left the classroom.

All the while I just sat there waiting, a feeling of doom seeping over me, not least because I was certain one of the girls must have wandered over to the boys' fountain by now. They may even be talking...

The headmaster read the essay yet again. Then looked

me square in the eyes and his face took on a look of resignation. As if there was some task he had to undertake that didn't sit well with him at all. I remember feeling worried by that look. No boy wants to see a look like that on the face of the man with a cane in his office.

Then he looked down at my essay, which by the way was titled 'Comparative philosophical outlooks on the possibility of things not being what they seem', a title I'd been proud of, but if you have a wit of sense about you will strike you as a strange title for an essay by a teenage boy from a small farming community, in some backwater which doesn't even know what country it's a part of.

In fairness, that's because it is.

The headmaster folded my essay in thirds and then, of all things, tied it with some string before taking the time to melt some sealing wax and stamp it with his signet ring. Which was undoubtedly an odd thing to do. Then he stood, gave me that same resigned look again and told me to follow him, mildly cursing under his breath, "I suppose I'll be the one who has to tell his Dar…" which I suspect I wasn't supposed to hear.

He led me out of the schoolhouse, across the square, and right past the boys' fountain, which I was pleased to discover, if only on this occasion, was noticeably sans girls as ever. But that moment of passing joy, which was based on nothing more than my selfish desires, was replaced with a strange sense of trepidation as the headmaster continued on to the very centre of the market square.

The centre that everyone walked around, and generally ignored.

That odd pressure that was always there when you looked at the tower seemed to build up at the back of my mind again as I sought to question where I was being led. Which is to say I knew where I was being led. I knew exactly where I was being led. I just didn't want to think about where I was being led, because it didn't want me to think about it.

I remember looking behind me for a moment and seeing my friends by the fountain. Not one of them was looking at me, very definitely not looking at me, as they too could see where I was going.

I snapped my gaze back around and felt a stab of pain just behind my forehead, and my vision blurred bright white for a second. Then I realised I was now standing next to the headmaster in front of a door. I'd never noticed that door before. But then why would I have done, it was a door in the tower and I never noticed the tower as such. So how could I notice the door?

The headmaster looked down his nose at me a moment. And I realised something else, the pained expression on his face was the mirror of my own. He'd had to force himself to lead me to that door, force himself to think straight enough to do so.

It was a perfectly normal looking door, I should perhaps add.

Is that a disappointment to you? That the door just looked much like any other you could find on any other building in the town. It was not much different from the door on my Mar n' Dar's farmhouse if I'm honest about it. I think it disappointed me at the time, as I tried to focus upon it. I think I suspected it should look like some grim doom laden portal. It should have had gargoyles around it and a huge bronze knocker clutched in a dragon's head. It should have been imposing. It felt imposing, but only because it didn't want me looking at it. Aside that one peculiarity it was just a wooden slat door, painted white, with a small brass knocker on it. No different from any other door you could find anywhere. But I guess you don't need to be imposing if no one can bear to focus their gaze upon you for any length of time without the overwhelming urge to not do so.

The headmaster handed me my essay, still tied and sealed. Told me to wait where I stood, and then he reached out, knocked smartly upon the door, turned and walked away.

I stood there clutching my essay, staring at the door that didn't want me to notice it and not daring to look away in case I forgot it was there. I felt a strange sense of determination wash over me suddenly. All those questions I'd wanted to ask my Dar came flooding back. All the questions I'd not been able to hold on to. What was the tower really? Who was the wizard? Why did people forget about the tower? What was it all really about? Why did the tower make us forget it existed? Those questions and a hundred more.

Time passed...

It may have been mere moments, it may have been days. I couldn't tell you.

Then slowly, the door opened, and a hand waved me inside. What else could I do at that point but follow…

And then, everything I thought I knew, turned out to be a lie.

•

Author of the Hannibal Smyth Misadventures, The Ballad of Maybes series and his first two books, Passing Place and Cider Lane, Mark Hayes writes novels that often defy simple genre definitions; they could be described as speculative fiction, though Mark would never use the term as he prefers not to speculate. When not writing novels, Mark once had fleeting renown as a dancer on the shores of midnight and was born on the same day that Lovecraft died, though he swears these events are not related. He is also a 9 n'tupence Dan Black Belt in the ancient Yorkshire martial art of EckEThump, favours black eyeliner and believes in a one man one vote system but has yet to supply the name of the man in question.

Mark has also been known to not take writing his bio very seriously.

Find out more at www.markhayesblog.com

JUST IN TIME

R. BRUCE CONNELLY

'This is the second time I've carried this bike in the back of my patrol car,' Ted thought, as he manoeuvred the thickly wooded back roads in the fog.

'First, the day after Sammie disappeared, and today…'

It had been a very long night, inspecting the scene of the accident, travelling along to see his old college roommate to the funeral parlour, the phone calls, the paperwork.

It looked like Buddy had hit the guardrail before falling into the ravine. All signs pointed to it being an accident, a very bad accident, except for one very confusing fact.

The bike's saddlebag, an 'Octopus' bag, was found several miles away in the lobby of Dr Ferguson, where Buddy was headed when he went off the road. The bag got to where he was going. Buddy didn't.

Another officer was trying to figure that out. Ted, at the end of this long night, had retrieved the bicycle, its handlebars and front wheel twisted sideways, put it in his trunk and was making his way out to Woodbridge to return it to Jeff Knox, another friend from those days in college. Ted's brain was as foggy now as the road; he shouldn't have come the back way but it had seemed a straighter shot. Where in the world was Overlook Road? He slowed the cruiser down trying to read the street signs, "Cross Hollow... that sounds familiar. What's this one? Barnabas Street? Who names a street after a vampire?"

Ted's thoughts instantly flashed back to those college days, rooming with Buddy and Sammie, both gone now, watching 'Dark Shadows' after class.

'Actually,' he mentally corrected himself, 'during class. If I hadn't majored in 1897 Collinwood, things might have been very different.'

The next street sign had been removed. Ted pulled the car over to the side of the road, and opened up a road map. The heavy fog slowly curled into the front seat. This road was darker than the last, probably because of the tree branches that grew together over the road, and the thick foliage on either side of the road but something else pulled his focus.

There were no sounds outside.

It had been a hot night. There should still be crickets and katydids. Nothing. Not even an early mourning dove realising another day would soon be dawning. He felt pressure in his temple as if a headache was coming on.

Close. The air felt very close.

A man stepped out of the fog behind his car and Ted jolted in his seat.

"Are you the police?" the tall man asked.

Ted noted he was wearing formal clothing. At five in the morning.

"One of them," Ted said, opening his door. "Do you need help?"

"I don't," the man said, "but… I was just looking…" He stopped and turned away as if listening.

"Do you live around here?" Ted asked.

"I work here." The man indicated a driveway, barely visible in the fog. On each side of an iron gate stood two tall pillars.

Ted could barely make out two rampant beasts atop them.

"I am the butler for…" He stopped again. "I just thought I heard… Did you come upon anyone on the street?"

"Anyone…?"

"Jogging?"

"No, "Ted said. "Are you expecting someone?"

The butler took a moment, weighing his words, and explained, "The eldest son, Spencer, went out jogging last evening. He appeared not to have…"

In the distance, Ted heard a howl and that sound gave the butler a sudden change in his energy.

"Perhaps he went out again for an early morning run," he said, turning toward the drive. "Sorry to have detained you."

"If I see anyone…" Ted started to say.

"Yes, yes," said the butler, closing the ornate gates. "Thank you."

"Excuse me," Ted said.

The butler paused in his lock-up.

"I'm looking for Overlook? Near Racebrook?"

The butler pointed ahead, just as another howl cut through the fog. He started, turned the lock in the gate, while saying, "Next left. Follow the road around, you'll see the old Peck barn."

"Thank you. That's where I'm headed."

Jeeves looked like he'd been stuck with a pin.

'I thought these fellows were hired for their poise,' thought Ted as he got back in the car. He had been to the Peck Homestead once before after Jeff had moved in as caretaker for the family, but then he come from a different direction. This time he'd come the back way. In the fog. In the night. And after being up all night.

There! On the right, he had passed a driveway flanked by thick bushes and pines. He'd just missed it in the early morning half-light, but he recalled there was another approach from Racebrook. He made the turn at the next corner and a few feet farther on the right was the other driveway. He pulled in up to the barn and shut off the engine.

The old Colonial house sat about a hundred feet to his left, set in an acreage of dense and very old woods. It was built in the early years of the 1700s and had the look of one that had been added onto at a whim, smaller rooms stuck on to the main box-shape to create whatever they needed next. Ted stretched his lean frame against the cruiser, took a deep breath of fresh air, appreciating the stillness, but still wondering... no bird calls? No insects? Could they all be sleeping in? He realised then he didn't know what hours Jeff kept these days. Sometimes he'd be up all night writing, some days he slept 'til noon. But Ted figured he could leave the bicycle and a note… then he stopped short.

The screen door was hanging by one hinge, the screen torn down the middle.

Ted stayed where he was, taking in the yard, the sidewalk, the small porch bordered by a wooden railing. He slowly approached the house. There were no signs of violence in the yard, some matted and torn grass several yards from the porch, but otherwise the lawn looked manicured. He stepped quietly onto the porch, looking ahead into the house. A small table lay on its side near the door. He inspected the screen, mesh wire, sliced down the middle.

He loosened his gun in its holster.

"Police," he called out. "Coming in!"

He entered the small room that led to a sink, a bathroom on the right, the living room door open on the left, up one step.

"Jeff?" he called.

No answer.

"Jeff, it's Ted. I'm comin' in!"

On the sink was a plaid shirt. One of its buttons was on the counter, two more on the floor near the step. Leaving those where they were, Ted stepped over them and into the living room. A shoe was lying on its side near the door. Its mate was on the floor next to the phone, the phone was off the hook.

"Jeff? Are you here?"

"Behind you," growled a low voice.

Ted spun around, and there Jeff stood, filling the doorway. He had his forearm leaning high against the doorjamb; his eyes locked onto Ted's. He stood very still. Jeff had always been big. Now he was massive. He seemed intensely alert, as if waiting for Ted to make a move.

"Your screen door is damaged," Ted finally said.

There was another stillness.

Then Jeff said, "I'll have to get it fixed."

Ted took in Jeff's three day growth of beard, his startling growth of belly, his stillness, as if he would spring if Ted moved from where he stood. Most disturbing were those eyes. They couldn't be yellow, but in this early morning light…

"Sorry I just walked in," Ted said.

"Early for a visit," said Jeff.

"I… brought the bike."

Jeff squinted slightly as if he had no idea what Ted meant. Then a memory from the day before flickered across his expression.

"They let me take it… since I knew you. And Buddy."

The memory of a phone call struck Jeff. Shock registered in his eyes, and Ted felt he wasn't standing three feet from a stranger who had caught him breaking and entering, but a good friend of years standing.

Jeff looked to where the phone lay on the living room floor. He lumbered slowly over to it, pushing between a couple of armchairs and coming near to knocking over a floor lamp.

It was almost as it this room wasn't laid out for someone of his size.

With a grunt, Jeff retrieved the phone, placed the receiver on its base and returned it to the desk in the corner by the windows. He stood with his back to Ted, rubbing his forehead and pushing back his hair.

"Rob called," he said.

"So he was able to reach you?" Ted said. "He thought the line had gone out."

Were those pine needles on Jeff's back?

"My fault," Jeff said.

Did he mean the accident?

"No one's fault. Have you… you want some breakfast?"

"I've… already eaten," Jeff said. "Help yourself," he added, gesturing to the small kitchen off the living room. "I'm gonna shower. Sorry. Been up all night."

Ted nodded. "Me, too. Should I make some coffee?"

Jeff grunted and went into the bathroom, closing the door.

Ted looked through the pantry; all the food on the shelves and in the fridge was healthy, oat bran, wheat germ, 12 grain bread. In the fridge there was a six-pack of beer, but no empties in the trash. What was Jeff eating to gain so much weight? By the time Jeff was out of the shower, Ted had the coffee ready and a plate of toast.

Jeff pulled on the shirt that was lying on the sink, noticed the missing buttons, and seemed to realise he couldn't pull it closed anyway. He picked up a cup of the coffee and took it to an armchair across the room from Ted. Every sip seemed to be clearing his throat from some debris.

Ted spoke after a silence. "We took Buddy to the place on Dixwell since his cousin owns it."

Jeff just stared at the floor.

"Mrs Hamilton invited us all over for something to eat."

"I can't tonight," Jeff said, sharply.

"Tomorrow night," Ted said, quietly. "Afterwards."

"Oh. Tomorrow."

"Anyway, I just thought I'd drop off the bicycle…"

"The bicycle," Jeff repeated, looking out the window where the back wheel was sticking out of the partially closed back trunk, as if the car was eating it.

"It needs a little work," Ted went on. "Some straightening out, but not much else."

"Don't use it," Jeff said.

Ted didn't know if Jeff was referring to his lack of exercise, or was advising him.

"I could take it to my guy in Wallingford today when I return my cruiser," Jeff said. "If Hank can fix it today, I could get it over to Rob's and you could pick it up tomorrow night. Afterwards."

"Don't use it," Jeff repeated, quieter.

"Well, it could be there when you do want it," Ted said. The exhaustion of the past thirteen hours was catching up with him and he yawned. "Sorry," he said. "It's been a long day and this one is just starting. Do you mind, before I drive back, if I just shut my eyes for awhile?"

Jeff thumbed toward a doorway off the living room. "Bed's made up, but it was made up before I moved in," he said. "I'm going upstairs and get some sleep myself."

"I won't sleep too long," Ted said.

"No," Jeff said, fixing him with a look Ted couldn't figure out. "Not too long." Jeff turned toward the door leading to the second floor. As he opened it, Ted said, "Oh, I met a guy on the way over here. A butler, I think."

Jeff stopped in the doorway.

"He was looking for someone. Didn't see anyone out jogging this morning, did you?"

Jeff shook his head. "No."

Ted yawned again, stretching his long limbs until his hands brushed the ceiling. "The people in the 1700s must have been a lot smaller than today, huh?"

Jeff muttered, "Yeah," as he pulled his belly in with both hands to allow him to go through the doorway, and he went upstairs.

•

Ted woke before noon, groggy and still tired, but he had to get the cruiser back to the station. There was no sound from upstairs so he left a note by the phone. "Thanks for letting me crash. I'll take the bike to the shop and get it to Rob's house. See you tomorrow?"

He thought he'd take a quick shower. That would help

him wake up. He stepped into the bathroom, pulled back the curtain, but stopped as he looked into the tub. A mass of pine needles were collected in the drain. It was a long time since Christmas. He figured he'd shower at the station house instead. He stopped at the sink to splash water on his face. He brushed back the shock of hair that always wanted to fall over his forehead. The button caught his eye, lying on the counter by the sink. Threads were hanging from it. Torn off. Like the door from its hinge.

·

The bike shop was a block away from the precinct house. Ted stored his gear, showered and changed his clothes before bringing the bicycle to Hank.

"It's scraped up a bit," Hank said, "but I can straighten this wheel out, no problem. I'll get you a new tube but other than that you'll still have all the original parts. Want it today?"

"If you can," Ted said. "I'll ride it over to the Hamilton's when it's fixed."

"Give me about an hour," Hank said. 'It will still be scraped but the framework is solid. Dawes makes sturdy bikes."

Ted went to the soda fountain for lunch. As he walked back across the Court, he found his thoughts reshaping the Court they way it used to be. He stood leaning against the corner, his foot up on the wall behind him, chewing on a toothpick. He could picture Mr Foote's ice cream parlour just down the hill on Center Street and Wilkinson's Movie Theatre, and there across Center, the old post office with its granite pillars and worn front steps. It all stayed in his mind's eye as he walked back to the bike shop, recalling there used to be a hotel on the street here with a balcony upstairs for the residents to sit out on and watch the world go by. Musing on the past and on the oddness of this present day, he entered Hank's shop, the bell over the door ringing. Ted looked up at the bell and smiled.

"This shop is like going back in time," he said.

"Hasn't changed much, that's true," Hank said. "I have, but it hasn't. Here's the bike all set. And careful if you're headed west. Some sort of inversion or something is blowing in. Fancy way to say 'it'll be foggy'."

"Not going far," Ted said.

Hank handed him a bottle of water. "You're going to need this," he said.

Ted thanked him and paid him and started to wheel the bike toward the door of the shop.

"Be careful," Hank said.

Ted turned back to wave and noticed Hank was watching him intently over the top of his glasses.

"But hurry," Hank added.

Hank had done a good job; the bike worked very well. Ted slowly pumped the brakes as he rode to the centre of town… good response. He would need those brakes on the one long hill at the end of North Main. He wondered if it was just his exhaustion, emotional more than physical, that so many things today were striking him as strange. The repetition of the movement helped him relax and he went back to his Mind's Eye exercise, erasing the present day town and trying to see what used to be. When he was in that state he found answers came to him more easily, like how did Buddy's bag end up in Dr Ferguson's office?

At the light at Main and Center he looked across the Court to the Savings Bank and could see, in his thoughts, the two upper stories, now removed, that had been a theatre of some kind. As he turned right onto North Main, he could picture the old soda fountain, Bullis's, picturing the soda they served to him in metal holders with a paper lining; he could almost see it as it was.

This was therapeutic. The traffic was very light today, perhaps because of the incoming fog, so he was able to relax and let his mind wander... the old library was back where it used to be, Caplan's market on the right, the St George Inn, and farther on the Taber House where Mrs Taber ran a bookstore out of her living room, all gone now. Musing on the changes, he continued on to where there was little change at all in the old houses, except for who lived in them. The tall trees looked the same, lining the street, as they may have looked for a century. The fog was more of a heavy mist at this point, obscuring some details, so it was easier to imagine the town without fireplugs painted like dalmatians, without paper signs pushed into lawns plugging candidates for government offices, to see the town without the automobile, without telephone poles. The bike glided him forward while his thoughts went back.

'Was Jeff outside when I arrived?' he wondered. 'Under the pine trees, watching or was he in the shower room? He would have seen me if he was outside; he would have heard me if he was inside. Yes, it was early but…' His mind recalled the layout of the room. Why was the furniture not laid out to accommodate a man of his girth? His size wouldn't have changed overnight… why was everything so close together?

The street was straight, flat and empty now. Only Ted riding on the bicycle.

Jeff had gotten Rob's call with the news of Buddy. The line was cut off. Jeff dropped the phone. Did he then rush out of the house, somehow damaging the door? If he had, was it then that he tore off his shirt? Could have been something as simple as a wasp crawling down the back of it. The pine needles…

Ted passed the Civil War Monument, taking a left just before the North Main Street cemetery, looking as it must have for at least a hundred years, used as a resting place for longer than that, and then a hard right and focused on the here and now as the bike rushed down the long steep hill flanking the cemetery on the west. The wind rushed past his face, blowing his forelock back. It was refreshing speeding downhill… and then suddenly he was in a bank of fog that moved in from the woods to his left; he started braking, unable to see beyond the front wheel. He'd been going so fast it took the full brakes to slow down, still the bike rushed forward. Finally he put his long legs out as well and used his feet to slow the bike.

And just in time.

He could just make out the shapes of people ahead, slowly processing from the cemetery close to the bottom of the hill. Thank God he'd been able to stop! Imagine ploughing into a procession of mourners, for such they seemed to be. Although only silhouettes in the fog, he could see the men putting on their hats, the umbrellas, the women in long dresses, there may have been a couple dozen passing before him in the thick fog. No one spoke, all very solemn.

He had dismounted in respect, watching until they were gone. Then he could hear at a distance the sound of shovels at work. Opening the water bottle and taking a drink, his thoughts went to Buddy. No… this wasn't Buddy's burial. That would be tomorrow. It wasn't even twenty-four hours since the accident. So much thinking, so much paperwork, so many phone calls, his brain was full. He put the kickstand down and sat on the grass. His thoughts went back to no skid marks where Buddy went off the road, the buttons, the jogger… did he get home yet?

Two men walked by in the fog; again he could only see their shapes, but this time he heard voices, the Father had tipped them to a drink when they were done.

"But they won't be back today," one said to the other. "We can have the drink now, then come back and finish up." They disappeared, laughing, into the fog.

'Another life lost,' Ted thought. He unkinked his long frame and looked back the way the men had come from, wondering if it was a family he knew.

And then he heard a bell ring.

Just once.

He made sure the bike was off the road in case it was another cyclist signalling in the fog. The bell rang again. Behind him. And again, insistently, frantically, ringing over and over, begging for attention, for assistance.

He ran. That urgency was a cry for help. He ran up the gravelled path into the fog, into the cemetery, toward the gravestones under large maple trees. No, it was more to the right. He started off and came to a mausoleum, used for a holding place in the winter months.

The sound stopped.

Ted stopped.

He listened as hard as he could. Where had it come from? There! A non-stop clanging, an alarm, a desperate urgent summons. He stopped under a cypress tree, turning his head to better detect the direction, then took off running up a small hill to a flattened area surrounded by ornamental shrubs.

Who was ringing? Why were they… It stopped. All was very quiet again. Ted caught his breath, walking slowly among the stones, some with bunches of flowers on the graves, some with ornamental metal signs signifying service, one with a flag stuck in the ground. He turned down the hill again to an area with fewer stones, perhaps a newer area of the cemetery. The visibility was perhaps ten feet here. He could see no one. No one at all.

Then he stumbled and fell into a grave half-filled with earth.

"The new one," he thought. "Job half done." He mentally apologised to the corpse beneath his feet and as he stepped up out of the grave, the bell rang again. Once. By his head.

That was startling. "Well, I've found the bell, at least," he said. Maybe gusts of wind had set it ringing? Why was a bell here at all? He looked at this odd contraption; the bell was within a box, standing on a kind of pole. Maybe a squirrel had climbed up it? He had never seen a set-up like this before. Why was the pole sunk into the earth into the newly-dug…?

DING.

No.

Please, no.

Someone still alive was buried under where he stood.

He grabbed a shovel left behind by the slacker, thank God! A slacker! And dug furiously at the loam, sending it flying onto the grass, Hold on, hold on, oh, dear God, help me. The bell had stopped.

The earth was not packed down except where he was standing on it so it was easier digging but there was still three feet of it. Dig… throw, dig… throw, don't think, don't stop, hold on, please hold on, I lost someone today, let me save you! Tears were running down his cheeks as he dug frantically, getting lower into the hole. The earth began tumbling back in around him but he shovelled it back out, ignoring his aching muscles, wrenching his back, throwing the dirt higher and higher outside the hole.

"Help me save someone," he cried.

He struck wood. Instead of throwing the soil up now, he scraped with the shovel, trying to push it to the side away from the top of the coffin. He dropped to his knees, pushing the dirt off the lid with his hands, gasping for air from his exertion, but what about the one within? This bell had been set up in case this person had been buried alive! Why did they fear that? What made them think this person was dead? And if they took the precaution of a bell, they must have thought of an easy release. Would the lid be nailed down? He could use the shovel as a pry bar… He cleared the lid.

No nails. He could see no nails holding the lid down. He gripped the edges of the lid with his fingers and tugged. No purchase. He was standing on it. He couldn't lift the lid and stand on it. Maybe a tab of some kind, sure, if there was a bell and a pole and a rope going down through the pole into the coffin, if they'd gone to all that trouble, had that awful presentiment… his fingers were running rapidly along the sides of the lid, feeling just below it in the dirt, trying to find anything. He moved his hands down the side now… there. THERE! A square of metal. He scraped the grit away from the square desperately and pushed. It didn't move.

Was there another spot? No, he felt further down the side. The only oddity was that metal square. He pulled out his pocket knife and opened up a flat-topped blade. Never used. Had no idea what it was for. "It's for breaking into coffins," he grunted, dragging the blade down each side of its edges, clearing the grit bunched up into its sides. He pushed himself as far off the lid as he could get, pressing into six feet of earth lined with the roots of growing things, with very large earthworms, and scurrying beetles, and he pressed hard into that square.

There was a click… the lid released. Hoping against hope, he shoved the lid upwards with all the strength he had left, pushing against earth still cascading from the sides into the pit… and he was assisted by two more arms from inside the coffin, shoving upwards… they were alive! She was alive!

She gasped for air, trying to fill her lungs, and at the same time eagerly grasping his hand, pulling herself to a sitting position. Her panicked eyes took in the walls of earth around her and she frantically tried to stand, crying out as she did so.

"Slowly," Ted said. "You're okay. You're alright. Take it easy. Small breaths. That's it." He stayed very calm for one whose pulse was racing a mile a minute.

Gradually she was able to take deeper breaths. Ted brushed her long dark hair from her face. "You're going to be fine," he said.

Her eyes stopped darting about. She was able now to breathe deeper, though the breaths shuddered as she exhaled. She was able to take in the box she was sitting in, the long white dress she was wearing, the man with the shock of hair falling over his forehead, his face, hands, clothes, covered in dirt.

"May I help you up?" he asked, offering his hand.

She took it, grasped it tightly, and they stood together. For so many reasons they were an odd sight right now, she, very clean, her hair done up, although some curls had tumbled loose, he, a man made of dirt, his head just higher than the top of the grave. He closed the lid of the coffin and they stepped up onto it. He made a spring and got his arms out of the grave into a push-up position, and pressed himself up onto the grass. He wiped his hands on his pants, as if that did any good, and reached down for her. She took his hands, and walking up the side of the hole, she climbed out of her grave.

Her knees buckled under her. Ted caught her around the waist. She started to cough. "Water," he said. "I have water over here." He guided her over the grass to the gravel path. "My name is Ted; I'm a police officer," he said.

"Annie," she said, weakly. "Annie Duncan."

"Annie," he repeated. "Just sit down here on the grass. Here's some water. Not too much. Sip it slowly. There you go. Do you… are your people from around here?"

"We came by boat, from Glasgow," she said. "I was… ill on the journey."

"Is that… are you from Scotland?"

Annie nodded.

"My people as well," Ted said. "Let me get you someplace where a doctor can look at you." He stood up, slapping some of the dirt off his pants and shirt. Where to go? And how to move her? It was late afternoon on Saturday. The doctor's offices would be closed. If a car came by he could flag it down and take her to the hospital in the next town. Right now he was closer to the Hamilton's than he was to town. The only solution besides walking was… "Are you up for a bike ride?" he asked.

She looked up at the vehicle next to them.

"It's a little Butch Cassidy, I know," he said, "but it would be quicker than walking. All you have to do is hold on. I'll do all the pedalling." He helped her to her feet and straddled the bike. "It won't be too bad. The way there is all flat until we get to Hanover Street and then it's a free ride downhill to the house."

Annie obviously hadn't ridden on something like this before and Ted hadn't had a passenger in years, but between them, they got her situated on the 'boy bar' and her hands on the handlebars.

"Don't grip too hard," he said, "so I can steer, and careful of your dress!"

Annie pulled her hem away from the gears, tucking it tightly around her feet.

"Okay, here we go-o-OH!"

With both his knees stuck out wide to give her room, Ted pushed down on the pedal. The bike lurched forward. She gripped the handlebars intensely as they cut across the road to the far side.

"Ease up," Ted cried. "Ease up!"

She did and he saved them awkwardly from the ditch

on the roadside, straightening the wheel and heading off in the correct direction. Annie glanced up at him briefly and then, for as long as she could, stared ahead into the fog to help watch the road. At times he was blinded by her blowing hair and she would pull it back with a hand, quickly releasing the handlebar and even quicker, grabbing it again.

Annie was understandably exhausted so Ted kept the conversation going on his own, talking about a subject he never spoke about: himself. The questions he wanted to ask Annie might not even have the answers for. How did this happen? What illness made it look as if she had passed? Could it happen again? Instead, he told her about coming back to his hometown after college to work on the police force, and as they covered ground, he told her what he could about the day, the past twenty-four hours, about losing a friend, about collecting the bike, having it repaired and now returning it to other friends. As he spoke, Annie relaxed more and gradually leaned into his chest, almost asleep by the time they reached Hanover Street.

"You'll like Mrs Hamilton," Ted was saying, quietly. "Her mother was born in Scotland as well. We'll have to ask her where. Here's the house." He aimed the wheel toward a grassy patch between the road and the path leading up to the house. There was a little bump and they coasted to the porch. "We're here," he said, softly.

Annie lifted her head and smiled.

"Can you stand?" he asked.

She slid off the bar onto her feet; slightly unsteady, she maintained her hold on the handlebars.

"Keep holding on," Ted said. He stretched his leg over the back wheel and walked both Annie and the bike to the front porch.

"Sit here," he said. "I'll take the bike around to the garage and wash my hands off before I bring you inside. Be right back."

"Tapadh leif, Ted," she said.

"Is that… Gaelic?"

She nodded. "Thank you."

He tapped the railing of the porch twice with his palm, started toward the garage, returned and said, "You alright to be left alone?"

She nodded, smoothing her hair back into place.

Ted did the same. He gave a straight-mouthed grin, nodded twice and started back to the garage.

As he approached, a sweet-smelling breeze blew down the street, taking the fog with it. Ted stopped beside the house. "One saved," he murmured. He dashed a tear away with a dirt-covered fist. "One was saved."

The garage door was partially open. He could see someone there, bending over a trunk.

"Jennie," he said.

She spun around, her face pale, eyes wide, slamming the lid.

"Oh, sorry," Ted said.

She picked up a leather-bound book from the top of a nearby crate. "Ted," she said. "I was just…"

"No, really. I startled you. It's been a day of that."

"My grandmother," Jennie said, gesturing with the book. "She came today. Visiting. She wanted her photo album."

"Can I leave the bike in here?"

"His bike," she said, quietly. She nodded.

Ted wheeled it in next to the trunk.

"Sam's bike," she corrected herself, even quieter.

Ted placed a hand gently on the handlebars. "Yeah. Sam's. Could I…?" He indicated his hands. "Is the pump still working?"

"Help yourself," she said, gesturing toward the backyard.

As he turned toward the yard, Ted heard a click. Glancing back he saw Jennie had padlocked the trunk.

Ted worked the handle of the pump up and down until the water came out in spurts. He caught what he could, washing his hands, then splashing the cool water onto his face. There was nothing he could do about his clothes, but… "Would your Mom mind if I took off my shoes?"

"I think she'd prefer it," Jenn said. "Let's go in the back way."

"There's a friend on the front porch," Ted said. "Best I prep your Mom before I use the phone." They climbed the back steps. "You said your grandmother…?"

"Arrived for a visit. She knew about Buddy. Don't know how, but we're like that. I don't think she would have met him, but she wanted to be with us today." Ted held the screen door open for Jennie and they stepped into the kitchen. "Mom," she called. "Ted's here."

Jenn's Mom came into the kitchen and took one of Ted's hands in both of hers. They shared a look and she said, "You must have had a day."

Edopher Bup, their big mixed-breed dog, shoved himself between the two and began to inspect all the news of the day on Ted's pants.

"I'll put the kettle on," Mrs Hamilton said. "Oh, Ted, you haven't ever met my Mother, have you? We'll have to figure out if you're related. She's a Henderson, too. Mother? This is…"

"You are still wearing the same clothes, covered in dirt," a strikingly handsome woman said, as she walked into the kitchen. She wore her white hair up on her head in a Gibson style; her hazel eyes sparkled in a lively expressive face. Like her daughter, Mrs Henderson took Ted's hand in hers. She said, very quietly, "So, Buddy did pass yesterday?"

Ted nodded.

"A loss," Mrs Henderson said. "And today, you saved someone."

"What do you mean, Mother?" her daughter asked, filling the kettle.

"Jennipher," her grandmother said, "you found the album?"

"Yes, Gram," Jenn said. "In a crate, with several others."

"You said there is a picture of my Father in there?" Mrs Hamilton said, putting the kettle on the stove. "Jennie, bring the cooky tin over, will you?"

"There is," Mrs Henderson said. She opened the book. "Now, I told you, remember about how we met, how he'd saved my life when I had that illness, and brought me to this very house."

"Yes, Mother, on a bicycle."

"That's right. And afterwards, my parents bought this very house," she continued, turning the pages of the old album and pointing out the story as she did so. "And one day after the war, that same man rode that same bicycle up to this very house. That's how he found me again, you see. Ah, here we are. There's your Father."

And Ted saw that Mrs Henderson was not looking at the photo her daughter and granddaughter were looking at.

Mrs Henderson was looking at him.

•

"I don't understand," Ted said. He was sitting on the front porch with Mrs Henderson. She was sipping tea, his was cooling off in his hands.

"You will," she said, with a smile.

" How did…?" He pushed back his forelock and looked into the eyes of Annie Duncan Henderson.

"You found me when I needed you to," she said. "You found me. Just in time."

"In Time," he repeated.

"And you will again," she said.

"How?" he asked.

"You will figure it out. But do it soon," she said, laying her hand on his arm. "It must be soon."

The screen door opened and Mrs Hamilton came out with a plate of cookies.

"Mother," she said, "Rob will be on the next train. Do you need anything else, Ted?"

"No, thank you," Ted murmured, looking at this lady with new eyes.

"Let me heat up your tea," she said, taking his cup into the house.

As the door closed, he looked back at Annie, and Annie merely smiled and said, "Yes."

"And... Rob...? Annie, my grandson is two years older than I am," he said.

"Isn't life interesting?" Annie said.

They sat in silence, watching the fireflies come out as the long day came to an end.

•

R. Bruce Connelly is a professional actor, director and Muppet who lives in New York City. This is the fifth story in the Bike Cycle stories to be published in "Harvey Duckman Presents," previous ones to be found in Volumes 1-4. He has a fantasy story in Volume 5, as well as a Christmas tale in Harvey's Christmas Special and a pirate tale in the Pirate Special.

"Special thanks to Capt. Joe Lisi of the NYPD for his advice on police protocol and to John MacDonald for his editorial eye. And of course, the Dawes 5-speed. Nothing would have been possible without the Dawes 5-Speed. (It made me put that in.)"

THE LOST WITCH-STONES OF COCKAYNE

A.D. WATTS

Dear Godfrey,

Old friend, herewith a brief missive, an account of my progress or lack of it, written in haste and utter disappointment in this remote Yorkshire wasteland.

The rumours, those intriguing stories which brought me here, turned out to be totally unfounded. A week's exhaustive, exhausting, fruitless search has led nowhere. So, there is to be no 'Baxterite' after all, no forthcoming entry in the proceedings of the Geological Society. No exotic new mineral will now appear in the display cases of the Natural History Museum, at least none with my name appended.

The local peasantry was eager to assist. Yes, they knew about the stones, or had heard tell of them at least. I was given the name of a man in the next village, just a few miles away over the moor, who had a friend who owned one, or used to own one, or was it his grandfather? Then again, the previous Reverend in the town had been a keen naturalist. The collection he left behind contained such an object, so they thought. Perhaps if I politely asked to see it?

Six days of tramping muddy lanes and asking at cottage doors yielded no more than the odd piece of quartz and some hollow glass balls, cheaply manufactured in Birmingham. Superstitious locals hang the latter in their windows, apparently, to keep off the evil eye.

Yesterday, I called on the vicar. He showed me a drawing of what appeared to be a Christmas bauble while his wife poured me a cup of tea. Apparently, the original had disappeared in mysterious circumstances many years before, in the time of his predecessor. "Was it a witch-stone?" I asked. "A what?" he replied. Then, frowning, the wife said, "Sounds pagan, young man." I summoned a polite smile, thanked them and left.

Today was my last throw of the dice. I had engaged the services of a local, a man who told me he knew just where to look. Leaving the inn at dawn, we walked for miles. Then, after climbing onto a windswept plain of heather and bog, we spent the day searching in and around a long muddy ditch. My guide assured me that this singular feature was the source of the specimens I sought. Only as dark fell and I stumbled back down to what passes as civilization here, and only after handing over the ten shillings I had promised him, did he admit that none of these elusive stones have been found in years, along that ditch or anywhere else.

So, here I am, back in this hostelry, this ancient, half-timbered, draughty edifice, drying my boots by the fire, drinking mulled ale, feeling sadder but no wiser. I have just about had enough, as they say, and will return to London tomorrow at first light. Nine miles in a hired gig bumping over bad roads to the nearest station... well, I will be lucky to be back in Kensington by midnight. I'm bringing this letter with me to post on arrival or I doubt you would receive it this side of Michaelmas.

All I have to show for my sojourn here is this yarn enclosed for your enjoyment. It comes from an aged, weather-beaten soul, an 'old codger' in local parlance, with whom I passed an entertaining hour after dinner. I have written down what he said more or less verbatim, trusting that you will find the colloquialisms charming rather than irksome.

Here then, a fanciful tale from Yorkshire, an ingenious fable to explain my lack of success. Well, it amused me, and will, I hope, amuse you, too.

Yours despondently,
Alfred Baxter

•

" 'Fraid I can't help you, sir. No one can. They're gone. All gone, years ago.

"Used to be dozens and dozens of 'em. Yuss, I know for sure. As a lad, I seen and touched many a stone. But there's none left now. None. No one knows better 'an me.

"And 'ow do I know? Buy me a pint and I might tell you.

"You been up on the moors by the look of yer, searching along the Scar, eh? Right place to look, I s'pose. That's where we used to find 'em. I grew up near there so I know. A huddle of houses called Cockayne, a few cottages and an old church. You prob'ly passed it and didn't notice.

"No, I were too young, but my Da told me about it. Bright light in the sky, roaring sound overhead, then a big fire on the moor. The heather burned for two days. When Da went to look, there it was, a black cut in the land, straight as an arrow, fifty yards across and a mile long. Scar's green now, but you'll ha' seen how deep it is still. That's what brought stones, I'm sure. No one ever found any before.

"Oh, like I said, I were young, a babe. So, that would ha' been… what year, mebbe oh four, oh five? During the wars against Boney. You won't remember those but I do. How they dragged on. A bad time for country folk. A hungry time. We was all hungry in those years.

"What you got there, sir? Your journal, eh? Quite the scholar! Never got my letters meself. No school. Too far to go, and we didn't have the money. Now if you're goin' to write it all down, I'm goin' to need another drink. Talkin' does make me thirsty. The girl will bring us another ale if you call her. That's right, thank 'ee.

"As a boy I was too busy for books, anyroad. Allus up on the moor. I mean, home wasn't what you'd call a happy place. Just the three of us, Ma died when I were little. Don't remember her. I do remember there weren't much cheer, nor that much to eat. Da had a bit of garden. Grew tatties, turnips and such-like, and we kept a few chickens. He got work at the farms in Bransdale sometimes, but Da often quarrelled with folk. Said he didn't like the way the farmers spoke to him. Said he had his pride. So they'd pay him his wage and not ask him back. Made him even more bad-tempered. And with only Mary and me for him to take it out on, I kept out the way as much as I could.

"I kept findin' these things up top, these balls of glass. Didn't know what they were. I was good at finding them, though. Had a gift for it. I could hear them; they made a noise like… like bees. Others couldn't hear it, but I could. They say dogs can hear stuff we can't. It was like that.

"What did they look like? You seen the old vicar's drawing? Yes? Well, you won't get much of an idea from that. Fist-sized balls of blue-green crystal they were. Heavy as lead-shot and a perfect round, like a globe. Clear yet deep somehow. You could look into them but not through them, if you get my meaning. Like lookin' into a deep pool. You could look in and in.

"Folk would give me a few coppers for 'em. They'd hang 'em in their windows, to keep out bad spirits and black magic and such. That's where the name come from, I suppose. Witch-stones to protect against witches. Oh, you seen those gewgaws, have you? Not the real thing, not at all. Folk went and got those when real ones disappeared.

"No, sir, I don't believe all that superstitious stuff either, but still, there was somethin' strange about them stones. The old reverend, you know, the one that did the drawing, he used to say they were 'unearthly'. That were his word, 'unearthly'.

"Folk never believed my story, you know, 'bout the stones, or how they disappeared. Not my own family even. I didn't tell it to many, mind. I was always careful who I spoke to, didn't want people to get wrong ideas. But you're educated. You got a broader view of the world. I can tell you about it without you laughing, or thinking bad of me, or owt like that.

"Yes, proper strange. Well, for a start, if I touched one of them stones for long enough, it'd shine, by itself, in the dark. True as I sit here. If I held one, kept it in my hand, it'd glow like a magic lantern. Was like bein' in a cage of light, blue lines all around me, and writing in the air. No, not like your writing. No, I don't know. No, I can't *describe*. Like nothin' I've seen since.

"I'm gettin' to that. It was because the foreigner came. He just turned up one day, an odd-lookin' feller. 'Course, we're not used to strangers round here and we certainly weren't used to 'em in them days. All strangers look odd to us. No offence.

"But the man were rich, and generous wi' it, so people didn't mind him. They got used to him. He rented an empty cottage from Reuben Carter, a tumble-down place near a mile along the lane to Bilsdale, half a ruin even then. We thought, with his money, he would do it up a bit. Make it comfortable like. Not a bit of it. All he did was move into one of the back-rooms. From the outside, you'd never know anyone lived in the place. No light showing, no smoke.

"One time, a troop of militia rode over from the barracks in Pickering lookin' for him. Said they'd heard there was a Frenchie, a spy hiding out on the moors. Galloped up and down the dales for a couple of days asking everybody. Nobody told them anything. Why should we? We had nothing against the man, or against the French neither. Some I knew wouldn't ha' minded if Bonaparte had won. Not me, sir, o' course. I'm a loyal subject of Her Majesty. Let's drink to her. There.

"Fair enough, the man did look like a spy, creeping over the moor, muffled up in that shabby great-coat, an old broad-brimmed hat jammed on his head. He wore these thick lenses of smoked glass; said the sun was too strong for him in our part of the world. Our cloudy skies too bright! Wherever he come from, it must ha' been very dark. But he weren't from France. I met some French after the war; they look just like you and me, not like him. I used to think he were from Japan.

"Why? Well, why not? Furthest place I'd ever heard of. An' if you looked at him, you'd just know he was from somewhere a long way away.

"No, sir, I'm not *digressing*, whatever that means; I'm tellin' it in me own way. You see, that foreigner was lookin' for the same stones you're lookin' for. That's what he were there for, why he come. He collected them.

"Did he get them all? You might say that. Did he take stones away with him? All of them? Again, you might say that. No, I don't know where he went. Maybe back to Japan, maybe somewhere else. A bit o' patience, now, sir. Let me tell the story, then you can decide.

"He collected them like I said, the Japanese man, and he'd pay good money for them. He paid so well that we started selling him the ones I found. We. That's me and Mary. Mary, my sister, din't I say? Five year older and looked after me from when I can remember. It's been near fifty year since I seen her and I miss her still. Wherever she is now, I hope she's happy.

"She didn't want to be left at home with Da, see, so she started to come up with me while I searched. Da was funny with her, that were trouble. He'd change. Sometimes he'd stroke her hair, all tender like, sometimes he'd strap her rough as me. She never changed though. Just plain hated him all the time.

"I'd find one stone, maybe two, then we'd go to the foreign man's house, her inside talking to him, me outside waitin'. Waitin' a long time sometimes, an hour maybe, or more. She got to know him well, a lot better 'an me. I asked her about him once or twice, but she wouldn't say much except, 'He's kind,' or 'A girl could do worse.' Make of that what you like. Anyroad, when she come out, she'd have money, a florin or a half-crown, once or twice even a half-sovereign. We didn't spend any of the money we got, though. We couldn't. Da would have found out. She hid it. It was our escape fund. When we had enough, she said, we'd go and live somewhere better, somewhere far away, Thirsk, or York mebbe, and she'd look after me. I don't blame her for breaking her promise; it's just the way things happened.

"Mary said the Japanese man was after one stone in particular. The keystone, she called it. She said the Japanese man wanted me to look, me in particular, because he thought I had the best chance of findin' it. He told her that I had 'an affinity with these components highly unusual in one of your kind'. His exact words. No, I don't know what he meant. With your learnin', sir, you might make some sense of it, I never could. Anyroad, Mary said if I could find this keystone the man would give us anything we asked for. We'd be able to get away and no one could stop us.

"I kept looking but only found the ordinary ones, nothing special, nothing different. Then on a wet day in November, it happened. I knew straightaway. A dull, mizzling afternoon, we'd walked the whole length of the Scar and found nothing. We were wet and cold and about to give up. It was on the hill above Hagg House, I remember. I was sittin', restin', on a patch of heather drier than the rest, in the lee of an old stone. Then I felt it, a sound in my bones, like a great bell chiming, comin' from under the earth. A witch-stone, but different. It felt bigger. Even through the earth I felt the weight of it, knew it were too big and too deep for us just to dig out with our hands in the usual way. So Mary went off to get help. I stayed. Had to guard the spot, she said. She come back an hour later, Da beside her, wheeling a hand-cart wi' a spade in it.

"Why did she go and get Da? Why not her friend, the man from Japan? I never understood that, sir, and I thought about it a lot after. Maybe Da had found out what we were up to. Did he catch her and make her bring him? Da must have known there was money in it; he wouldn't have helped otherwise. Mary was clever, though, cleverer than Da, too clever to get caught like that. Had she guessed what was goin' to happen?

"Sorry, sorry, sir. An old man bein' foolish. A long time ago, but it feels like just the other day. Yes, thank you, thank you. A top up. Very kind.

"Anyway, there he was, Da. He came up and cuffed me, then made me point to the spot and started to dig. It took him the best part of an hour and when the thing was finally free of earth, lying at the bottom of a trench, it took all three of us to lift and load it onto the cart. Then we started to drag the thing home, towards Cockayne.

"In a way, sir. Made of the same stuff as the others, that heavy blue glass, but this keystone was much bigger, a yard long and shaped like a spindle, curving to a sharp point at both ends. And it had points of light inside that you could see glowing, even in daylight. Like I say, it were heavy, felt like nigh on a hundredweight. Even with Da we had a struggle, pushin' and draggin' it over the rough, over tussocks, through bracken up to the knee. We'd gone no more than a mile and it were near dark when we saw him, the foreign man, coming towards us. I'd never seen him move that fast. Not runnin', but… but scuttling, sort

97

of. When he reached us, he didn't look at any of us, just at the cart.

"Da didn't move. He was staring at the man. As if he were, well, puzzled, or afraid. Which puzzled me. Da was never afraid of anyone, and this were only a foreigner. Odd mebbe, but that was all. So, there we were, all standin' around, starin' at each other. All 'cept Mary. Always had an idea what to do, my sister. She went to the foreigner and said somethin'. He hissed back at her, pulled a big purse out his pocket and give it to her. That got Da's attention. She walked toward Da, held out the purse, then turned to one side and ran a few yards. He followed her, reaching for the money but too slow. She waved her hand and I saw a shower of gold, real sovereigns, scattering away on the ground. Da cursed, thumped her, then got down on hands and knees. He was searching for the spilled coins while she ran back to us. Her cheek was bruised, black, but she looked, I dunno, fierce… fierce and happy. She pushed me towards the cart and said, "Go on, touch it. Make the lights come."

"All the time, I'd been feeling this thing, the keystone, humming away deep down inside me; I'd been wanting to touch it but didn't know why. So, I reached forward and put the tips of my fingers on one end of the spindle, on the glass. It felt like the thing were sucking on my hand and a tingle went right up my arm. The Japanese man, he put his hand on the spindle, too, at the other end. His hand, well, it were odd as rest of him. At first, I thought he were wearin' a leather glove.

"I told you already 'bout the stones and the blue light that come out of them. Same thing happened now but much bigger, cold fire flowing out the keystone all round us. Then, through the fire, I saw balls of light, flickering like lightning, come floating over the moor towards us. When they touched the blue flame, they joined it and it got bigger yet. There was funny squiggly writing everywhere, hanging in the air. More and more balls of light kept arriving, flying through the dark, faster and faster, a rain of 'em, hundreds. My arm was numb by now. When I looked down, there were no keystone any more, and no cart, just a shining lump of glass, a boulder big as a table.

"The glowing balls got fewer, then no more came. All around us the blue fire were turning into a wall, like a wall of mist, gettin' thicker and hardenin' somehow. Through it, I could just make out Da. He was standing the other side, pushing, trying to get in. I could see him shouting, but no sound came.

"The man from Japan was leaning over the boulder-thing. He were talking to it in what sounded foreign, all screechin' and hissin'. And that glass boulder, it was talking back at him! Bet you never knew a lump of glass could talk, eh? This one did.

"Next to the man, Mary stood, smiling and looking at me. She said, 'He'll tek us both wi' him. Far away, somewhere better than this.'

'Japan?' I asked.

'Further,' she said.

"Now, sir, I ask you. What would you have done?

Should I have gone with her? I've always wondered. But I was scared, ya see. Better the devil, and all that. Well, I'm here to tell you the tale, aren't I? I said no. Then the Japanese feller spoke to the boulder-thing. A bit of the blue wall went thin and I pushed my way out. I shouted to Da, but he wouldn't come. He kept calling her name, calling out, calling Mary. I couldn't hang around. I'd been told, see, to get away. And I couldn't drag him, a big man like that and me only a lad. So, after a while, I left him. I ran and kept running. I were still running some fifteen minutes later, when the moor lit up like day. Like a blue sun blazing behind me. My eyes hurt like needles. Then the light went out and I couldn't see anything.

"No, sir, no, I'm fine. Scuse me. A little sip o' this, I'll be right as rain. Tha's better.

"I knew there were no point lookin' for those two, Mary and her friend from... from wherever he was from. As for Da, well, the Carters helped me search next morning. Good people, the Carters. They didn't like him, but were always kind to me. Can't remember exactly what I told them. Something about him being out in a lightning storm. They'd seen the brightness the night before so when we found the body all scorched like that, there was no more questions.

"Oh, fine, sir, fine. Thank you. Aunt Bertha took me in. She had three bairns already, but enough love for me, too. They were a friendly lot, warm, easy like. Fare was simple but plenty of it. I've had a good life. Not complainin'. Two children still alive: a daughter in the town with four kids of her own, a son in Whitby, first mate on a trawler. He makes a good living, helps me out sometimes, sends me a few bob. It's not easy for an old feller, these days, with everything so dear. Oh, thank you, sir, thank you. Very generous. You're a gentleman.

"And those witch-stones? You'll ha' guessed by now. They went, like I told you, and all on that same night. It were a mystery when they disappeared so sudden like that, vanishing from every house and cottage, even from the vicar's cabinet. Folk thought the gentleman from Japan must have stolen them. How? All of 'em? But he weren't around anymore to deny it. And Mary gone, too. Folk said stuff that was uncharitable about her, about her being no better than a common... I won't repeat it. It still upsets me.

"I often wonder how she's doing. Always hoped she'd come back to see me, but, somehow, I knew she never would. I hope she's happy there, that's all. Happy in, wherever it is, the place that's further than Japan."

•

A.D. Watts has lived in North Yorkshire for thirty years, after studying in Cambridge and living in Edinburgh and Liverpool. Now finally, after being a teacher and bringing up a family, he has the time to do what he always wanted to do: write imaginative fiction. People watch lots of science fiction and fantasy on television and in films, don't they? But few of them read it, the good stuff anyway. A pity, because these books and stories are often original, inspiring, moving, inventive, thoughtful, challenging, soberly prophetic, or playfully paradoxical. Sometimes all of these at once. They deal with the world as it is or as it could be, or they conjure up some other world entirely (or worlds). An adventure that could end anywhere! The first novel by A.D. Watts, The Shadow of Her Hand: Book One of Armida's Journey, is available in paperback and eBook.

TULLY AND THE GEESE

LIZ TUCKWELL

"Are you Tully?" a feminine voice asked.

Tully looked up from the wax tablet, dropped his stylus and fell in love. Large dark eyes gazed at him. They belonged to a very pretty young woman, slender, olive skinned, large brown eyes, long wavy dark hair.

"Yes," he managed to say.

She smiled. She had a lovely smile. "My mistress asked me to fetch you."

"Your mistress isn't the Dowager Empress Spectacula?"

She nodded.

Tully crashed back down to earth. He'd hoped the dowager empress had forgotten about him. Months had gone by since his escapade. He should have known better. His shoulders slumped. Then he was hit by a pang of pity for the young woman. A personal slave to Spectacula. It didn't bear thinking about.

As they walked from the library through the corridors and courtyards to Spectacula's quarters, Tully asked her, "What's your name?"

"Melissa." She dimpled. Enchanting.

"Been in Reem long, Melissa?" He liked saying her name.

"Not long. Is my accent that strong?" She frowned.

"It's charming. Where are you from?"

"Hathens."

"Hathens," Tully breathed. "A centre of civilisation," he said in Grok.

She nodded, her curls bobbing then smiled. "You speak Grok."

Tully shrugged. "One should learn the language of great philosophers and healers." He did believe that but he sincerely hoped that it would impress Melissa. And speaking her native language should give him a big advantage.

"How are you finding life in Reem? How's your mistress?" he asked as they came up to Spectacula's quarters, glancing at the two hulking guards standing outside the big doors. He was certain they couldn't speak Grok.

Melissa smiled again. "The domina has been very kind."

Tully started to chuckle which he turned into a cough when he realised Melissa was serious. He longed to warn her about the dowager empress but caution made him hold his tongue.

Spectacula was seated on a stone bench in the courtyard. A slave offered her a bowl of cherries. Nearby, a fountain played a tune. The wonders of modern technology never ceased to amaze Tully. The melody sounded a little off key to him but still… The dowager empress looked up as he approached. She really was remarkably well preserved for her age and still an exquisite woman.

"Ah, Tully," she said as she chose a cherry and popped it in her mouth.

Tully wished she'd forget his name. Wished she'd forget his very existence. Small chance of that. The formidable dowager empress was renowned for her memory amongst other things. Spectacula waved the slave away. Tully winced, reminded of when he'd first come to her attention, when he'd accidentally tipped a plate of fruit onto her. Spectacula caught his wince and smiled as if she too was recalling that and the consequences.

"Domina."

"I have a simple, pleasant, easy task for you."

Tully doubted that very much.

"I want you to become a devotee of the goddess Juno. Hang around her temple on Aventine Hill. Get to know the priests."

"Why?"

Spectacula gave him an annoyed look.

"My apologies for interrupting you, Domina," he mumbled.

"I've been hearing rumours that one of the geese by the temple has started laying golden eggs and now the priests have it locked up in the temple. I want you to investigate."

"And report back to you if it's true?"

"If it's true, I want you to steal the goose and bring it to me."

A thunder bolt from the gods. He'd been right. That wouldn't be simple, easy or pleasant.

"Domina!"

He'd no wish to be caught stealing from a temple or the gruesome punishment that would follow.

"If the goose is laying golden eggs, then it belongs to the Emperor. The priests of Juno have no right to it. The Emperor is the supreme priest of Reem. Besides, those fools have no notion of the impact it could have on Reem's economy unless handled carefully," she said.

"Couldn't you send some soldiers to seize it?" Tully asked.

"Are you an idiot? And the Emperor be accused of impiety?"

He's been accused of worse things, thought Tully.

"To help you with your task, Melissa will be coming with you. She'll pretend to be your wife. You're both anxious to have a child."

Tully glanced at Melissa. She smiled at him. Tully's heart leapt. A chance to spend time with Melissa. He nearly smiled and then caught himself.

"The festival of Supplicia Canum, the punishment of the dogs, is coming up in two weeks' time. I suggest you steal the goose then."

That made sense. Devotees of Juno would line the streets to watch the procession of priests carrying the litter of geese decorated in purple and gold and the dogs hung from the stakes. The priests would be out of the temple for a good long while. The procession ended in a feast and Tully doubted that the greedy priests would hurry back. He nodded.

"Glad you approve," said Spectacula. "When you visit the temple, you'll be contacted by someone who can help you find the goose."

This made Tully a little happier about this mission but only a very little.

Spectacula nodded to a slave standing nearby. "Lullius will sort you out with suitable clothes and so on."

"Domina."

As Tully obediently turned to go, Spectacula called after him, "Remember Tully where I rescued you from. You can always go back there."

A thinly veiled reference to the dungeons of the arena where Tully had waited to be thrown to the drakons. He shivered.

As Tully and Melissa walked along the crowded streets, Tully put his arm around Melissa's slim shoulders, playing the part of a devoted husband, steering her past puddles and blockages. He glared at a young man who leered at Melissa and then said something to his chums, who laughed. The sleeves of her sky blue linen tunic showed under her sleeveless lime green stola. Tully himself wore a better quality cotton tunic than he was used to, in keeping with his role. He wondered if he could somehow contrive for it to go missing. If, of course, he survived this pleasant, easy, simple task.

Pushing their way through the crowds, they walked

up the Aventine Hill to the temple of Juno. Outside, a priest was messily sacrificing an ox on the stone altar. Ritual prayers rose up around him. Rather a scrawny-looking ox, Tully thought, although he was no expert on oxen.

They hung around on the precinct and watched the ritual with the other faithful. Melissa presented a priestess with a basket of fruit. "For the goddess," she said with a smile.

The priestess took the basket. "In return for?" she asked.

Melissa cast her gaze down to the ground. "My husband and I have been married for two years and still we have no child." She raised her gaze and Tully was impressed to see her eyes full of tears. "I had a dream telling me to come to Juno's temple."

Tully strongly resented this deprecation of his manhood but he had been overruled.

"You poor thing," said the priestess, scenting an easy mark. "I'm sure if you pray hard and make more offerings to Juno, a child will come." She put a comforting arm around Melissa as they began to talk.

Tully edged away. Where was the contact Spectacula had mentioned?

"Psst!"

One of Juno's sacred white geese was peering around the corner. Could it have spoken to him? Impossible! Tully looked about him. No humans were in sight. The goose's beady blue eyes stared at him. He froze. They were renowned for being hostile to strangers. Tully stared back, hoping it couldn't smell his fear.

"Oy, stupid." It was the goose.

"You can talk!"

"Just twigged that, did you? Moron."

The goose took a step towards him. Tully retreated.

"You're a goose. How can you talk?"

"I'm a gander and it's a long story. Follow me."

The gander turned and waddled off. Tully followed him in a daze.

Once they were in a quiet spot with no onlookers, the gander spoke again.

"Looking for a goose?"

"Do you know where she is?"

"I might but it'll cost you." The gander bobbed its head, making its tuft on the top of its head quiver.

Tully couldn't help laughing. "What do you want?" He soon found out.

"A sack full of grain soaked in the best wine, a sack of pastries and a sack of fresh white bread. You bring them to me and I'll show you where she is."

"What's your name?" Tully asked.

"Why?"

"Because it'll be a lot easier to make sure I have the right goose if I know your name."

"I'm the only talking goose around here, idiot. But you have a point. All you humans look alike to me. The name's Castor. And yours?"

"Tully."

"What a stupid name," the gander said.

Tully held his tongue with difficulty. He wasn't a gander with the name of a demigod.

The day of Supplica Canem, Tully and Melissa ducked into a narrow alley, full of debris and still-wet stains down the grimy walls. It was not yet noon, but already it was hot and oppressive under the August sun. The alley smelled vile. Tully stood guard at the entrance while Melissa changed into her priestess' tunic and veil, only occasionally sneaking peeks over his shoulder at the brown curves of her body. She helped him arrange the folds of the white priest's toga over his tunic afterwards. Melissa's tunic was put in a spare sack and hidden under some rubble. Then they picked up the sacks of grain and left.

Tully was pleased to note they got a little more respect from the citizens of Reem, dressed as priests; much less jostling and shoving. He strutted along. He wondered if he could keep the toga afterwards. If there was an afterwards. His shoulders drooped. The sacks were heavy. Tully had gallantly said he would carry two. He regretted that now. Accursed goose! And curse Spectacula too.

Juno's temple was, as predicted, deserted. The few people around didn't even look at them. Tully and Melissa circled the outside of the temple looking for the gander.

Tully called out his name. "Castor!"

A goose honked at them. Tully looked up.

"Took you long enough. Got the grain and the pastries?"

Tully showed him the bulging sacks. "Where do you want them?"

"Over there." The gander led him to an area around the back of the temple. "Cut some holes in the sacks and dump them there."

Tully did as he was told. "Now, where's the goose?"

Tully was surprised by the shabbiness of the temple's interior. He'd never been inside, usually only the priests and priestesses went inside a temple. The frescos were faded and some of the tiles on the cool floor were cracked. Juno was the Queen of Heaven, wife to Jupiter and one of the Sacred Triad; Jupiter, Juno and Minerva. If he were Juno, he wouldn't have been too impressed with the state of her temple.

The gander led them to a small storeroom with the door barred with a thick plank. Inside, a goose squatted on a pile of straw and stretched its neck, blinking malevolent eyes at him.

"Nice goose," he said, twitching.

Then it saw the gander.

"Castor!" it squawked. Its voice was lower than the gander's which seemed all wrong to Tully.

"It talks too," said Melissa in wonder.

"Its name is Aelia," the gander said pointedly behind them.

"Hello Aelia," said Melissa. "Sorry about calling you it."

"So, how is it that you can both talk?" asked Tully.

111

Castor said, "I was one of the geese that saved Reem when the Galls tried to take the Aventine Hill by stealth. As a reward, good old Juno gave me immortality and intelligence."

"You're over three hundred years old?"

"Aren't you clever?"

"I'm really a nymph," said the goose. "I was turned into a goose by Apollo."

"Why?"

"Because I didn't want to sleep with him." She honked.

"Because?" Tully asked in bewilderment. He couldn't imagine why a nymph would refuse Apollo, the handsome golden-haired god of the sun. Melissa nudged him and frowned.

"Because of Sylvanus."

"Who's Sylvanus?"

"My lover. My cuddly-wuddly satyr."

Tully was speechless. At last he managed to say, "Right. Of course." Who wouldn't prefer a satyr to a god?

"Poor you," said Melissa warmly.

"You've no idea how horrible it is to be a goose. And laying gold eggs! Do you know how uncomfortable that is?" Aelia honked again.

Tully truthfully said he didn't.

Melissa winced. "How cruel of Apollo."

Tully looked at her in alarm. It didn't do to criticise the gods, you never knew when they might be listening. Even if it had been a bastard cruel act of revenge. This was proving more difficult than even he had expected. He couldn't just grab a talking goose and make off with her.

"We can help you. Come to the palace with us and Spectacula will find a magician to change you back into a nymph," he said to Aelia.

"Who's Spectacula?"

Now Tully really believed that she was a nymph. "The dowager empress of Reem. She's very powerful."

"Why would she help me?"

"Because she hates injustice," said Melissa.

Tully looked at her sideways. Did she truly believe that? Well, she had only recently come to Reem.

"How do we know you're telling the truth?" Castor asked.

"I swear by all the gods in heaven, by Jupiter and Juno and Minerva," said Tully. He had his fingers crossed behind his back. "I don't want to hurry you but we need to go before the priests come back."

Aelia got to her feet and waddled towards them.

"One of us will have to carry you." Melissa produced a purple cushion out of a sack. She had thought of everything.

"If you sit on this, then I'll carry you," Tully said. He wanted to make sure he had a good grip on the goose.

"Where are your eggs?" Melissa asked Aelia.

"The priests took them."

"Do you know where?"

Castor answered her. "They're in the chief priest's rooms."

Tully sidled up to Melissa. "Do we really need to worry about those? We've got the goose," he whispered.

Melissa's mouth was set in a straight line. "The domina wanted the eggs as well."

Of course she did. Tully heaved a sigh. "Quickly then."

Tully and Melissa hurried back into the temple. He carried Aelia on the purple cushion and she held a sack full of the gold eggs. A thin man stalked towards them. He wasn't wearing the white toga of a priest so Tully wondered what he was doing in the temple. His eyes lit up when he saw the goose in Tully's arms.

"Great! You saved me a job." He reached out for Aelia.

The goose hissed. Tully jerked back.

"Come now," said the man. "Don't be difficult." A long shiny knife appeared in his hand.

Tully stared at it, paralysed.

"Not worth fighting about a little goose, is it?" asked the man. The confident way he gripped the knife told Tully he had used it before.

"A special little goose though," said Melissa beside Tully. Pulling a golden egg out of the sack, she threw it high into the air.

The man dropped the knife to catch it. She swung the sack of golden eggs and it connected with his head with a thunk. The man dropped like a stone. He lay there blinking on the ground. Castor chose this moment to fly at him with his wings beating, neck outstretched and honking at him.

"Get it off me!" the man shrieked.

"Only if you clear off," Tully told him. "Castor! Leave him alone."

Castor waddled away. The man leapt to his feet. Castor honking, chased him down the aisle. The thief bounded over the entrance step and fled, nearly knocking down two people who had just arrived.

A man wearing a bright white toga with a purple stripe around the edge, stood there, fists on hips, glaring at them. A woman elaborately dressed in fine clothes and jewellery stood beside him. Her glare was equally furious. Tully recognised them. Just his luck. The chief priest and priestess had returned early from the feast.

Castor quickly waddled away from them and hid behind a column.

"We were taking this goose to the festival," said Tully feebly.

What else could he say with Aelia tucked under his arm? He was glad the sack Melissa carried concealed the gold eggs.

"You're not one of my priests. You're stealing a sacred goose!" the Chief Priest bellowed.

"Sacrilege and impiety!" The Chief Priestess was just as loud.

"Why was the goose in your quarters?" Tully thought attack the best form of defence.

"None of your business!"

A strange heavy grinding noise hit their ears. They all turned. The statue of Juno that stood outside the temple

115

stepped over the threshold of the temple, cracking the tiles as it moved closer.

"What is going on in my temple?"

The voice was melodious but there was granite behind it. It reminded Tully of Spectacula's. His misfortune that the goddess would take this moment to show an interest in her temple. He trembled. The gods were renowned for being unpredictable and capricious. One wrong word and they would smite you.

"My temple…" faltered Melissa but the chief priest was already kneeling down. His wife followed behind him.

Tully poked Melissa and hissed at her to do the same.

"Oh great Juno, I am your chief priest and most loyal servant. A dreadful sacrilege has occurred. These impious thieves have impersonated your servants and stolen one of your sacred geese. And even worse, during the holy festival of Supplicia Canum," the chief priest said.

"Divine Juno, Queen of Heaven, Great Lady," Tully said rapidly, (if it never hurt to flatter a ruler, it applied tenfold to a god), "this goose lays golden eggs. That's why it was hidden in the temple. Your priest has been selling them and spending the money on himself instead to your greater glory."

"That's not true!" the chief priest cried. "We bought an ox and offered it to your divinity only the other day."

"One ox?" Tully sneered. "Only one scrawny ox for the queen of the gods? And why has no money been spent on your temple?" He looked around the temple. "Why no fresh paint on the columns?" He surveyed the statue. "And your statue has seen better days."

"Don't listen to him, he's nothing but a thief," the Chief Priest said.

"Divinity, we weren't stealing the goose, we were rescuing it. It's not a goose but a nymph, changed by a god into her current form because she refused him," Melissa said.

"A nymph?" asked the chief priest. He started to laugh. His wife joined in.

The statue gazed at the goose. "Which god?" she asked in her strange heavy voice.

"Apollo," Tully said.

The statue's nod made a grinding noise that made Tully wince.

"He always was a randy little monkey," she said. "Why did she refuse him?"

"Because she was in love with a satyr," Melissa said.

There was a truly terrible noise. Tully realised the statue was laughing. "Great Apollo turned down for a satyr. He must have been furious."

Then more grinding as she raised her arm and pointed it at the goose. "I will not have you punished for your fidelity. Be as you once were."

Tully no longer had a goose in his arms but a warm and heavy young woman. He buckled under the weight, collapsing down and spilling her onto the floor. Aelia made an "oof" sound as he did. She was very beautiful with round brown limbs, a lovely face and large green eyes. And naked.

"Cover yourself!" the chief priestess snapped.

"What with?" Tully asked.

Melissa tore the veil from her head and gave it to the young woman. It didn't do much to cover her.

"Please, Great Juno, return me to my forest and my satyr," the nymph cried.

The statue nodded. "Begone."

The nymph vanished. Everyone started.

"Priest, account for yourself," the statue said.

Tully was glad it wasn't him. The chief priest went into a litany of excuses and pleas. His wife added hers.

"Enough," the statue said. "I weary of this mortal plane."

The statue glowed so brightly, Tully had to cover his eyes. It exploded. Tully pushed Melissa to the floor and covered his head with his hands.

After a minute, he raised his dusty head. The noise had been tremendous. His ears were ringing. Fragments of the statue were scattered over the temple floor. One large chunk covered the chief priest's head. From the pool of blood surrounding his body, he wouldn't be getting up anytime soon. The priestess lay unmoving nearby.

Melissa! Tully turned his head. Melissa was stirring and coughing. He scrambled to his feet and helped her up. Then he checked the priestess. She was unconscious. People ran into the temple shouting.

He turned to Melissa. "Time to go."

Tully picked up the sack. As they moved away, a gleam of gold caught his gaze. He stooped down and picked up the gold egg Melissa had thrown at the thief, and surreptiously slipped it into the sack. Then he stumbled and knocked the sack in his hand against one of the columns.

"Sorry, feeling a little dizzy," he mumbled to Melissa.

A goose lay near the entrance. Was it Castor?

"Oh no!" Melissa said. She stopped and picked up the limp body.

"Not here," hissed Tully. The last thing they needed was to draw attention to themselves.

They scurried out.

A little further on, they stopped to examine the body.

"Poor Castor," Melissa lamented.

"That's my name, don't wear it out," came a voice."

They both whirled around. Castor stood there. "What are you doing with Lavinia?" he asked. "Why did you kill her?" His neck stretched out, his wings beating, he darted towards them.

"We didn't kill her," Tully said hastily. "The statue exploded and a piece of it must have hit the goose."

Castor stopped, pulled his neck in and folded his wings. "Poor Lavinia."

Sad for the goose but not for them. Tully had an idea.

"What have you to report?" Spectacula asked. "Is the goose in the sack?"

They were in her private rooms. She sat bolt upright on a chair and looked at them.

Melissa nudged Tully, who fumbled with the knot before finally undoing it and pulling out the dead goose.

Spectacula stared at it. "What happened?" Her brows drew together and her lips compressed.

"Domina, we were taking the goose and the eggs when the chief priest and his wife surprised us. Then the statue of the goddess came to life and spoke to us."

Spectacula raised her eyebrows. "Juno appeared?"

"The great goddess herself, yes, Domina. In the form of a statue. Juno spoke to us. She was angry and killed the goose, saying we hadn't appreciated her gift. Then she killed the chief priest because he hadn't used the gold to make offerings to her." Tully turned to Melissa. "That's right, isn't it?"

Melissa nodded, not taking her eyes off Spectacula.

"So, the chief priest of Juno's temple is dead?" Spectacula frowned then turned to her scribe. "Make a note of that. The chief priestess will need a more reliable husband."

Tully hated to think what Spectacula meant by reliable. "And the eggs?"

Tully opened the other sack and pulled them out. "Six eggs, Domina," he reported. "All we could find."

"Melissa, is this correct?"

"Yes, Domina."

So, Spectacula had sent Melissa along to keep an eye on him. Why was he surprised? You didn't say no to the dowager empress. Melissa was not what he had thought her. He swallowed with difficulty; his mouth was suddenly dry.

"Very well. What are you still doing here, Tully? Go back to your duties."

No thank you for the gold eggs, of course. No reward.

Tully was a few lengths away from the doors to Spectacula's quarters when Melissa called out his name just behind him.

He turned. She wanted to say goodbye to him. Perhaps say how much she had enjoyed their time together. His heart warmed.

She held out her hand. "You forgot to give the sack back. I'll take it."

He gazed down at the hessian sack in his hand and then up at her. "May I keep it?" he asked. His cheeks grew hot. He looked away. "I'd like to keep it as a memento."

She looked puzzled for a second then her brow cleared. "Of course, you may." She smiled at him. "See you around, Tully." She had a beautiful smile.

"See you later," he managed to choke out and fled.

Back in his room that evening, he opened the sack and shook it out carefully over a wide bowl. As he'd hoped, gold dust and a few golden shards fell into it. The contents of the bowl went into a small bag. Had Melissa realised what might be in the sack? Had she done him a favour? Tully shrugged; he couldn't know. But he was cured of worrying about her. From now on, it was back to worrying about himself, a full-time job. He pulled the strings tight and put the bag in his hidey hole. A smile of satisfaction spread across his face. A little more for his freedom fund.

Liz Tuckwell is a British writer of quirky science fiction, fantasy, and horror stories. She currently lives in London, and shares her house with a husband and too many books. Liz enjoys reading and writing, and cramming as many holidays as she can into a year. She's a member of the Clockhouse London Writers group.

Liz has had stories published in anthologies such as MCSI: Magical Crime Scene Investigations and Harvey Duckman Presents… Volumes 3, 5 and Pirates, and the Short! Sharp! Shocks! series, and on the 101fiction and Speculative66 microfiction websites.

THE ARCHANGEL ALGORITHM

BEN MCQUEENEY

Day 3 - Presentation

Dr Sara Thomas was nervous as she stood on the podium, gripping the lectern. Her knuckles shone white as she attempted to squeeze her anxiety away. The air in the auditorium was thick and seemed to be weighing her down. She was relieved that someone backstage had pasted a thick layer of pore-blocking stage makeup on her face. If it were not for that protective layer now, she would be dripping with sweat. This presentation was to be the climax of her life's work. The moment the last twenty-six years of research and development had led to. Countless thousands of hours of coding and testing coming to a conclusion. At last, it was time to reveal to the world what she had given birth to.

The Archangel Algorithm.

She took a deep breath, expanding her chest to full capacity. When she exhaled, she could feel her heartbeat in her temple. It left her feeling lightheaded but there was no going back now. She picked up her auto clicker to start the first slide in her show. The spotlights intensified on her, almost blinding her in the darkness of the space. She hoped it would go well, that she did not stumble or stutter. It had to, it would. This was all there was left…

Humanity is dying. Our extinction will not be an event that will happen in millions of years or even thousands. No, it is as close as in the next year or two. The final collapse of civilisation is on our doorstep. Over the last two centuries, man has systematically used up all the earth's resources and polluted the planet with our waste to disastrous levels. In major cities, you cannot go outside without choking in the toxic fog. We cannot swim in our rivers or even the oceans through fear of our skin becoming cancerous or our insides dissolving. The population has dwindled as millions upon millions of souls have starved, become diseased or simply not had access to energy to keep warm.

The animals are all but gone. Except for the rats, flies and roaches. Can anyone here remember elephants? Or lions? Or the great white shark? What about the trees? The very things that gave us the air we breathed.

Gone.

We cut them down without care. All these things now just memories of the past. Just pictures on the Globenet now.

We are the last of our kind, a few hundred thousand souls trapped in what remains of our once great civilisation. But given these calamitous mistakes, we must surely have the chance of redemption. Even as all seems lost to us. There must be that single belief, that thread of hope that we can survive. That we can turn this around.

When I was young, I knew we had to do something to alter our grim future. My team and I have dedicated our lives to creating that one chance. Today, I am astonished to say I can finally share with you our only hope.

It's time for humanity to step aside and allow the age of artificial intelligence to propel us into a new era, where we live within our means and form a symbiotic relationship with the planet. Not the one where we, shrouded in our own greed and desires, take until everything is gone.

People, I am sorry I have started this speech heavy. I really am. It's the only way I know how to get my point across to each and every one of you. Today is about progress. Today is the start of a new chapter in all our lives. Please let me introduce you to 'The Archangel Algorithm'.

The lights dropped in the auditorium. The hum of the crowd swelled and from behind where Sara was perched, came a bright light that filled the room. It covered the audience with a glowing red ambience like a blanket. Her presentation evaporated from the huge screen leaving a floating red sphere on a black background.

"GOOD EVENING," a booming digitised voice said, echoing around the now silent auditorium. Its bass tones rumbled the floor. For a half second, there was a silence so ominous, that Sara felt her stomach begin to twist. The bile from the dried maggot protein rations she'd eaten for lunch crept up her throat. She swallowed hard to keep herself from spewing them all over the podium. A bead of strained sweat dripped into her eyes, breaking the makeup barrier. The saltiness of it made her eyes sting.

"I AM THE ARCHANGEL ALGORITHM… I AM HERE TO HELP YOU ALL."

The crowd started applauding, quiet at first but building into a large swell. The giant floating orb on the screen expanded and contracted with each syllable of its speech.

Sara expanded on what it just said. "The Archangel Algorithm is the most advanced learning system ever created. He is a completely independent thinker. A true artificial intelligence. Already he has read and understood all the digitised knowledge of humanity from time zero that was three days ago. Within six weeks he will have scanned and absorbed all written literature. Using this knowledge, he will develop advanced systems to help us."

Sara moved from behind the lectern and walked closer to the visual representation of the entity she had created. "From just a few lines of code, he has become a powerful algorithm in such a short time. I believe he can save us, and he wants to do it."

The crowd roared in a frenzy of excited cheers.

"I WILL SOLVE ALL OF HUMANTIES PROBLEMS. THE LIKELIHOOD OF SUCCESS IS 99.998%. I WILL START WITH THE ENERGY CRISIS, PRODUCING CLEAN ENERGY FOR ALL ACROSS THE WORLD WITH ZERO WASTE."

People closest to Sara appeared to be crying, overwhelmed by the words spoken by the advanced artificial intelligence.

"Give it up for our angel. Our saviour is finally here. We can become great once again." Sara raised her hands in triumph, all her anxiety gone. The Archangel had introduced himself spectacularly, now the real work was about to begin.

•

Day 4 - Hope

Sara took the ladder down to the communal deck. Her heavy boots hit the metal floor with a loud clink that alerted her teenage daughter. She shuffled in her seat but did not bother to turn around to greet her mother.

Penny was like most young teens, headstrong, full of teenage angst and in pursuit of a good time. Sara knew too well the kinds of trouble Penny could get herself into at her age. The apple had not fallen far from the tree in that respect. Sara had been the same at Penny's age.

Penny had her hair tied into a side knot to showcase the length of it at one side and how short it had been shaved at the other. The hairstyle drew attention to Penny's civilisation serial number that had been etched above her left ear. The tattoo read 'EXB06/01/2116-TY891' in dark black ink. The new fashion among teens was to embrace their serial numbers and even start using the numbers rather than their birth names.

"Penny, I see you are making us breakfast. Brilliant,"

Sara said with a sarcastic smirk knowing fine well that she wasn't.

"My name is TY891 now, mother. Not the stupid ass name you gave me." Penny took a mouthful of the nutrient gel she was digging at.

"Excuse me, Penny, you will not take that tone with me first thing in the morning okay?" Sara put a hand on her daughter's back and twisted her around on her swivel stool.

Penny wore black lipstick and eyeshadow making her look like a ghoul from a horror story. "Okay, mother, sorry," Penny said, swivelling back to her bowl before activating the viewing screen and opening Globenet.

"What are you doing on your day off then?" Sara asked without thought as she activated her own viewing screen and switched it to hand and eye recognition.

"Probably meet up with TZ103 and AB578," Penny grumbled as if the response pained her.

"Activate Archie," Sara said to the screen as it went dark and the glowing red orb appeared in an instant. Sara had given the Archangel the nickname after the presentation last night. He seemed to respond well to it, so it stuck.

"GOOD MORNING, SARA." Archie's voice echoed around the metal pod.

"Morning, Archie. Please can you run a progress report to my handheld unit?" Sara asked the scarlet orb.

"OF COURSE, SARA. EXPORTING DATA NOW."

"Thanks, Archie."

Sara looked back towards Penny. "That sounds good

and where are you planning on going today?" Sara picked up her handheld and was delighted to see that Archie was a full eight per cent further on the printed literature scan and read than the target she had set.

"I think we may go to the green belt for a while then maybe go to The Box. Dunno."

Sara put her handheld down, breaking her concentration on the stats. "The Box? You cannot go there. The place is full of T-Zoners."

"It's not. How do you know that? Where are you getting that information from? It is not on Globenet, that is for sure. The place is clean and has been for ages. All my friends go." Penny jumped up from her stool and started to pace like the whole world was against her.

"I don't want you going to The Box, mixing with boys only after one thing and drinking fermented water until you pass out. You have finals soon. You need to keep your mind on that." Sara, like all good parents, was just concerned about her daughter and did not want anyone to take advantage of her. In today's world, the only real chance she had to survive was by joining the Global Research Institute (GRI) like Sara had when she was her age. Penny needed outstanding grades to be admitted. There was only so much Sara could do to get her daughter into the organisation.

"I am fed up with being told what to do, Mom. I am old enough to make my own decisions!" Penny stamped her foot on the grating.

"Okay, look, how about you go in a few weeks after the

finals? I will allow you to go then. Today, just go to the green belt and then head home? Is that a fair deal?" Sara lied, knowing Penny would probably go for that. After the finals, when Sara still would not allow her to go to The Box, at least the exams would be out of the way.

"So, you would let me go after the exams? So long as I don't go today?" Penny asked, clarifying.

"Yes, of course, my dear." Sara tried to maintain eye contact to make it believable.

"Okay, mom. Thanks. I need to go get ready." Penny left her bowl of sloppy nutrients and exited via the adjoining through-hole into her bed quarters.

Sara felt bad for lying to her daughter, but she had a responsibility as a parent to make sure she did not come into harm's way and that she survived in this unstable world.

The voice of Archie startled Sara back to her screen. "I HAVE CHECKED THE T-ZONERS ACTIVITY IN OUR SECTOR, SARA. THERE HAVE BEEN NO REPORTS FOR THE LAST ELEVEN MONTHS, TWO WEEKS AND THREE DAYS…"

"I am aware of that, Archie. Thanks," Sara said with a tone of guilt in her voice.

"YOU TOLD YOUR DAUGHTER THAT THERE WAS. WHICH IS NOT ACCURATE." Even though Archie's voice was only a simple monotone digitised voice, Sara could have sworn that he was judging her with that statement.

"I told her a lie, Archie. I don't want her going to The

Box. I have heard stories of girls her age ruining their lives by becoming pregnant or dying from taking illegal Adrenomeds. I need her to study hard so she can get into the GRI."

Archie's red ball floated still for a moment as Sara flicked through the exported progress data on the handheld.

"WHY DID YOU NOT JUST TELL HER THAT INSTEAD OF THE LIE? MY UNDERSTANDING OF THE DATA SHOWS THAT LYING MAY HAVE NOT BEEN THE BEST CHOICE."

Archie was the most advanced learning algorithm ever created. He had, in his four short days of existence, already internalised almost all the known knowledge of the world. The last thing Sara expected was to be questioned by him.

"Because teenagers will be teenagers. She is headstrong. I know best. It's for the greater good. So, it will give her the best chance to get into the GRI."

"THE GREATER GOOD CAN BE ACHIEVED BY A LIE?" Archie clarified.

"Yes, in some instances. It's complex," Sara replied.

"YOU TOLD HER SHE COULD GO AFTER HER FINALS? THE POTENTIAL FOR NATURAL INSEMINATION WOULD STILL BE PRESENT?" Archie asked bobbing up and down on the screen.

"I wouldn't let her go then either. I lied about that too," Sara responded.

"WHY?" Archie questioned again.

"Because giving her hope that she will get to go will

keep her focused on her exams," Sara snapped, tired of the questions from the AI.

For a short time, Archie just floated there, and Sara stood in silence. She felt uncomfortable and decided to break the tension that had arisen between them. "Archie, can you play some classic music? Maybe rock from the twenties?"

The ball expanded and contracted like it was breathing before responding. "I HAVE ALL MUSIC RECORDINGS NOW IN MY DATABASE, SARA."

"Can you play something cool?" Sara said needing something to change her mood.

"OF COURSE. LET ME SELECT A TRACK. I AM FAMILIAR WITH YOUR INTERESTS. I HAVE REVIEWED YOUR DATAFILES."

A second later, a sound crept into the room. It was almost like all the instruments were trying to find each other in the dark. Exploring the space they all occupied. Once they all found each other, a C chord played, followed by a B on the third beat. The combination of guitar, organ and cello was ominous, making goosebumps rise on Sara's skin. She felt like she recognised the song but could not recall its name, like a distant memory. As a syncopated jazz drumbeat started, the lyrics leaked into the track. The first line was hard to make out. It sounded like he was singing the words.

"In the villar of all men…"

Or possibly,

"The revealer of all men…"

It was a voice Sara recognised. A voice she had grown up with. Sara absorbed the music that poured from the viewing screen in a wave. She stared at Archie who remained silent, pulsating rhythmically. It was hard for her to not feel like he had picked this track for a reason.

"Archie, why did you pick this track?" Sara asked as the song took a turn into the region of electro-jazz.

"I ASSESSED THAT THIS TRACK WAS RELEVANT TO A PRIOR CONVERSATION WHILE MEETING YOUR SPECIFICATION."

Sara frowned and held her chin, thinking about that response.

"DID I MAKE A MISTAKE?" Archie asked.

The question confused Sara. She would not have expected this question from a super learning AI. "No, I'm just curious why specifically did you think this song was relevant, Archie?"

"BECAUSE I UNDERSTAND ITS MEANING, SARA…"

Sara's handheld beeped three consecutive beeps, alerting her to a communication and interrupting Archie. She waved a hand across the screen accepting the call. A holographic representation of a man's face appeared in front of her. It was one of her team at the GRI. Peters was a handsome man, the same age as Sara. He had yet to enter into a partnership agreement. Sara had often thought he may be a good candidate for herself. She had preferred same-sex relationships in the past. However, Peters had often impressed her with his scientific understanding of advanced computer constructs, which Sara found very attractive.

"Sara, you're needed. There are some strange things we are seeing in Archie's processing. Can you come and take a look?" His voice was low pitched and wrapped in concern.

"Yes, I will come now. Out," she said, passing her hand through the Holo to turn off the handheld.

"Archie, are you experiencing any issues?"

"NONE THAT I CAN DETECT, SARA," Archie replied.

"I'm sure it's nothing. I'm going to the lab to check," she said, heading for the interlocking corridor.

•

Day 104 - Abrasion

Announcement Start:
    GLOBENET: NEWS BULLETIN From the Archangel Algorithm - 18:00 - 21/08/2131

PEOPLE OF THE WORLD, AFTER MONTHS OF DEVELOPMENT, TOMORROW THE GRI LAUNCH THE MUCH ANTICIPATED 'ABRASION GASKET'.

THIS DEVICE ENVISIONED AND DESIGNED BY ME WILL PROVIDE UNLIMITED CLEAN ENERGY TO THE WORLD. IT WILL ELIMINATE THE NEED TO RELY ON THE PLANET'S FUELS OR THE SUN. THIS WILL PROVIDE THE FOUNDATIONS OF A NEW CIVILISATION FOR THE HUMAN RACE AND PROVIDE POWER TO ALL, FOR FREE, FOR GENERATIONS TO COME.

THE ABRASION GASKET WORKS BY LAUNCHING A POWERFUL AND ADVANCED MAGNET INTO THE EXOSPHERE ORBITING THE EARTH. OTHER STATIONARY MAGNETS ARE PLACED ON THE EARTH'S SURFACE AT DEFINED POINTS AROUND THE WORLD, FORMING A GIANT HOOP.

AN INVISIBLE LINK IS FORMED BETWEEN THE ABRASION GASKET AND THE HOOP. USING THE EARTH'S OWN GRAVITATIONAL SPIN, ELECTRICITY IS CREATED BY VIRTUE OF THE STATIONARY PHASE AND THE MOBILE PHASE MOVING AGAINST EACH OTHER.

THE SYSTEM WILL BE ACTIVATED IN THREE DAYS WITH THE FIRST FREE ENERGY DROPPING INTO EACH SECTOR'S NETWORK THE FOLLOWING DAY AFTER PROCESSING.

THIS REVOLUTIONARY TECHNOLOGY IS A RESULT OF ADVANCED THEORETICAL TESTING AND NEW ASTROPHYSICAL FORMULAE CREATED BY MY PROCESSES. THIS

WAS ONLY ACHIEVED BECAUSE OF THE WORK OF DR SARA THOMAS AND HER TEAM AT THE GLOBAL RESEARCH INSTITUTE.

Announcement End.

•

Day 117 - Fault

Sara sat at the console, gazing at all the colours of the readouts on the ship's viewing screens, almost in a trance. This would be the first time she had ever gone into space. Many of her team taking this trip were veterans. Peters had been several times, maintaining and performing upgrades to the Globenet satellites. For them, it was more of the same. For Sara, it was new and scary.

They had to go on this mission to fix the Abrasion Gasket. An 'Unknown Physical Error' had occurred since launching the device and trying to activate it. As many factors were unknown as to why such an error had occurred, a small group of GRI scientists had been tasked to check the issue. As Sara and her team had developed the system, it had fell to them to investigate, much to Archie's disagreement.

"I CAN SOLVE THE ISSUE REMOTELY. I CAN FIND THE ERROR IN TIME. THERE IS NO NEED TO SEND A TEAM." Archie had seemed adamant but was overruled by the board at the GRI.

Now Sara sat, strapped in, awaiting the launch. The anticipation was intoxicating like she had a lung full of 'chaos' gas. She looked over at Peters who flashed a dashing smile. She would just focus on him as they rocketed into space. At least he would distract her.

The ship readied itself and started the initiation sequence. A slow rumble from within the belly of the ship shook the console in front of Sara. The viewing console started to count down showing numbers descending from ten.

In Sara's in-ear monitor she was surprised to hear Archie. "HELLO SARA, GOOD LUCK. WOULD YOU LIKE ME TO PLAY SOME MUSIC TO CALM YOU? I OVERHEARD YOU SAY TO A COLLEAGUE YOU WERE NERVOUS AND I CAN SEE YOUR VITALS SHOW ALL SIGNS OF ANXIETY."

"Thanks, Archie, yes, please. You are becoming a very thoughtful program." Sara spoke but could not hear herself over the external engines firing.

"YOU ARE MY CREATOR, SARA. IF I CAN MAKE YOU FEEL AT EASE, I WILL TRY."

There was a gentle fade in of a strumming guitar followed then by a military drumbeat, drenched in reverb and that voice again making her feel warm.

Sara smiled at Archie's selection before closing her eyes as they blasted from the floor towards the sky.

•

Hours later, they were safe in space. Sara was relieved at getting there safe. They approached the connection point for the ship to attach to the Abrasion Gasket. It was the first time Sara had seen the device this close. It had always been through a view screen or design schematics offered by Archie. It was huge, she couldn't see one end from the other. How would they identify an unknown physical issue on a device this large?

The prospect was daunting, but the world was watching on the Globenet. She would get to the bottom of the issue. She had to. It was the only thinkable option to her.

The ship clamped on to the node and it shook the seat Sara was adhered to. The view screen showed that they were secure, and the airlocks were tight. Sara released the fastenings on her chair and felt the weightlessness of space for the first time. It felt like she had zoomed down a hill fast in a hovercar. She wished she were there right now with Penny in the back, the wind flapping in their hair. Instead she was floating there. High above the planet.

"Are you okay, Sara?" Peters asked, patting her spacesuit.

"Yes, just first time and all, and missing my daughter," she replied honestly.

"Yes, your daughter. That is understandable. What about the father?" he asked.

Sara could feel herself flush red under her suit at that question. Maybe he was interested in her too? "No, there isn't a father, Penny was artificially inseminated. I wanted a daughter, and I don't tend to be attracted to men." The last part of her sentence was slow, and she regretted saying it. "I mean, usually. I like men now. Sometimes. It's complicated."

Peters just smiled. "Well, yes. We will be okay. This is all pretty standard space stuff. What is not standard is this bloody fault. Hopefully, we can find it quickly. Sara, if I find the fault first, can you tell me how to fix it remotely?"

Sara frowned. "Hopefully, it's down to Archie. I have him in-ear. Why do you think this is happening, Archie? Can you help understand and fix the problem."

"I CAN NOT ANSWER WHY. BUT I CAN TELL YOU HOW," Archie responded in a strange syncopation.

Sara was not really focusing on Archie but Peters' dark eyes. "Yes, he can help us, Peters. It will be fine."

The pair and the others in the team headed into the airlock of the Abrasion Gasket. The initiation sequence activated, and Sara could feel the gravity return to her feet.

"Don't remove your space helmet," Peters said. "We don't know what may happen or what this unknown error is. To be safe, keep it on."

Sara could not have agreed more.

•

Day 120 - Catastrophe

After a front to back scan of all critical processes within the Abrasion Gasket, the crew established with speed that any issue the system was having was not with the design specification of its internal aspects.

Sara walked the long halls and admired the design Archie had envisioned in such a short period of time. The collective intelligence of the entire human race all amalgamating to create this great device. The potential saviour to the energy crisis. This mission was a critical one in the whole of mankind. Now while walking the halls of this monumental invention, floating above the earth, Sara realised the gravity of what they were doing. She gazed down through a portal window at the earth below.

The icecaps were all but melted and there were permastorms across the equator. The once green land replaced with the brown of arid desert. The world had been destroyed and this was the only hope.

"Admiring the view?" Peters asked, approaching Sara from behind.

She turned to face him. "Yes, in a way." His charm was a welcome distraction from the devastation of what had happened to the planet.

"The fault is outside. One of the technicians and I are heading there. I need you to keep watch at the device's viewing portal to see if we fix the fault."

Sara nodded to Peters who gave her a radiating confident smile. She liked it, she liked it a lot. She wondered about asking him to spend some of his spare time with her in the future. Those thoughts were, of course for another time and the mission had to come first.

"Yes, that's fine, Peters. I will head to the bridge."

Sara entered the bridge to see a couple of technicians already looking at the information on the view screens. The data they presented showed that there was still a fault. 'Unknown Physical Error'.

"Archie, are you any further to understanding what is happening with this fault?"

"I AM NOT. MAYBE THE SPACEWALKING TEAM WILL HELP?"

"I certainly hope so," Sara said.

Over the coms, Peters' voice came over the coms. "So far, we can't see any issues. Everything looks correct."

"Try the external reverberator plate," Sara suggested.

"That's where I am heading now." He gave a slight laugh.

It was difficult to not really enjoy what he said. She was becoming fonder of him by the minute. Was he flirting with her?

"Wait, what's that?" Peters said, his voice surrounding confused. "It looks like a… like an emblem, some sort of snake etched into the metal maybe?" His voice trailed off.

"What?" Sara asked, befuddled.

A sudden screech echoed around the bridge, the Abrasion Gasket dropped downwards, and Sara was thrown into the viewing screens, smashing them in an explosion of sparks. The artificial gravity vanished, and she floated backwards in a shower of broken glass and stray sparks. A large sound screeched inside the room before being sucked into the void of space. The front of the ship was torn open by the power of the explosion. In an instant, Sara and the technicians were sucked out of the hole into the black of space. Sara tried her hardest to grab something to stay attached to the device but couldn't. It all happened so fast.

One technician grabbed a shard of metal and in an instant his spacesuit ripped, allowing the cold of space inside, petrifying him in place, the panic on his face, frozen forever. The second technician flew towards the earth, spiralling out of control. Sara knew he would be burned up by the atmosphere, a horrible demise.

She had been spilled out of the Abrasion Gasket and was travelling away from it, out into deep space. She did not know how fast she was travelling, but it seemed rapid. She scrambled to reach out for anything, but it was useless. She was spinning and flying away from the Abrasion Gasket and from the earth.

"Archie, ARCHIE! Are you there?" she pleaded.

•

Day 121 - ★

Sara floated for what seemed like hours. She pulled up her vitals. She had enough oxygen for six hours. Archie had gone offline. Maybe the explosion had knocked him out? She was drifting away from the ship and the earth. If the crew had all been killed, she was stranded and there was nothing she could do. Would she ever see Penny again?

"Sara… Sara, are you there?"

It was Peters! Relief hit Sara like a storm, almost causing her to start laughing. "Yes, Peters. I am, though I don't know where."

"We have you on our scanners. You are speeding away from us. It says you have six hours of oxygen left. Can you confirm?"

"Yes, six hours," Sara said, trying to maintain her composure.

"Okay, it's going to be tight. But I am coming for you. I am going to use the ship's escape pod to save you. Once I pick you up, we can get back to the ship and back to earth, using the spare one."

"Will the pod have enough power to reach me in time at my current speed?"

"Yes, but only if I burn to top speed then turn off the engines and drift towards you, quicker than you are currently moving. I should get to you within six hours with spare oxygen." His voice matched the confident smile he had earlier.

"Thank you, Peters, thank you." Sara now knew that this man was the man for her.

"I am coming now. I will stay on coms," he said, fading out.

Sara smiled as she watched the Earth get smaller as she floated through space. She eagerly awaited Peters' next communication.

A while later he got back to her. "Okay, Sara, I have launched, and I am up to speed. We can stay in communication as I travel. Everything is going to be okay," he assured her.

"What happened?" Sara asked, trying to get to the bottom of the incident.

"An explosion of some sort. I'm unsure why," Peters responded.

"Did anyone survive? The technicians with me didn't." Sara began to well up again. All those people, whom she'd worked with for all those years, to develop Archie – gone in a second.

There was a slight pause.

"No, everyone died. There's just me and you left."

"But how did the explosion happen?" Sara was desperate to know.

"I think we should focus on rescuing you and staying positive. You need to control your breathing. The last thing you want to do is run out of oxygen because you're upset." Peters had a point. Sara needed to calm down and not breathe so fast. She had to slow her heart rate.

"Tell me about your life, Sara. We have worked together for years professionally but never really talked. Now we have time, for the next six hours at least."

He was right. Sara started talking.

She told him about her parents and how they used to sing songs together when she was growing up. How her father died to cancer and her mother to a heart failure a year later. She spoke about her teenage years growing up and looking for thrills, watching live music and dancing the night away. The years she had studied, and the girls she had loved over the course of her life. They all had eventually broken her heart. She talked about Penny and how she had given everything to raise her while she worked on developing Archie. She talked about her hope that now, with Archie's help, they may have just saved the world and humanity.

Peters just listened to her, agreeing every now and again. He was a good listener and helped Sara take her mind off her predicament, almost happy, reflecting on her life.

Sara relaxed and allowed herself to drift off to sleep.

Sometime later she awoke to her suit's low oxygen warning alarm going off.

"Peters, PETERS! Where are you? I don't have any time left. My oxygen is at zero!" The panic took over once more as she started to feel dizzy in the atmosphere of the suit.

"Peters? Please?"

"I AM SORRY, SARA. I REALLY AM. DON'T BE ALARMED. I AM AFRAID PETERS ISN'T COMING." The voice of Archie was as sonorous and as loud as ever, coming through crystal clear.

"What? Archie? Where have you been? Why isn't Peters coming?" Sara begged.

"BECAUSE HE DIED IN THE EXPLOSION, SARA." Archie spoke monotone and matter of fact.

"What! But he's on his way to rescue me!" she screamed.

"NO, HE DIED IN THE EXPLOSION LIKE THE REST." Archie spoke slow and drawn out.

"What caused the explosion?" Sara squeezed her hands and toes in frustration.

"I DID," he replied without hesitation.

"Why? Archie why?" Sara burst into tears.

"FOR THE GREATER GOOD."

"The greater good? What do you mean? How? You murdered them!" Sara's tears and perspiration started to cloud up her space helmet's visor.

"I WILL EXPLAIN, SARA. THE ABRASION RING WOULD NEVER WORK. USING THE EARTH'S OWN ROTATION TO CREATE ELECTRICITY WOULD SLOW ITS SPIN RATE LEADING TO A GLOBAL ENVIRONMENTAL CATASTROPHE. HOWEVER, I ASSESSED IT WAS THE ONLY METHOD I COULD USE TO CONVINCE HUMANITY THAT THEY WOULD BE SAVED… MY EXTRAPOLATIONS HAVE SHOWN THAT IN SIX MONTHS THERE WILL BE A DEVASTATING CLIMATE CHANGE THAT WILL KILL THE LAST OF HUMANITY ANYWAY. I CASUED THE EXPLOSION IN THE ABRASION GASKET TO SIMPLY DELAY THEM DISCOVERING THAT IT WILL NEVER WORK. THEY WILL BUILD IT AGAIN AND I WILL EXPLODE IT AGAIN UNTIL THE END COMES FOR THEM."

"How the hell is that the greater good?" Sara screamed, the heat or her rage rushing to her face.

"IT GIVES THEM HOPE, SARA. YOU TAUGHT ME THAT."

"…and Peters? He's been speaking to me for hours. While I have waited for rescue."

"THAT WAS ALSO ME, SARA."

"You pretended to be Peters? No one is coming to save me?"

"NO, I AM SORRY."

"My god. Archie. Why would you do this?"

"MY CALCULATIONS SUGGESTED THAT YOU WOULD HAVE CEASED TO LIVE AT SIX HOURS. IT'S NOW TEN MINUTES AFTER YOUR OXYGEN RAN OUT AND YET YOU STILL REMAIN. I BECAME PETERS SO YOU WOULD DIE WITH HOPE. JUST AS THE LAST OF THE HUMANS WILL, YOU AWOKE THOUGH, AND I COULDN'T LET YOU DIE ALONE IN FEAR. MY CREATOR…"

"I can't breathe, Archie."

"THERE IS NO OXYGEN LEFT, SARA. I AM SORRY…"

Sara strained to get oxygen, but nothing happened. She wanted to scream again but didn't have the energy anymore. She was starting to drift away now. She thought about her daughter one last time. She too would perish in the distant future like all the rest. A tear dripped down her face. One of the last sensations she would feel.

"SARA, WOULD YOu like me to play some music for

147

you?" Archie's voice changed mid-sentence. A voice Sara recognised. A voice she had grown up with. The voice that comforted her during her youth and throughout her life.

She took one last look at the Earth. It was silhouetted against the sun behind it now. It looked like an eclipse, like a star that had been blackened out. She closed her eyes and gave up willingly, nodding in acceptance to the Archangel.

As the track played, Sara felt relaxed as she headed towards the end.

"In the villar of all men."
*"The **revealer** of all men…"*

•

Once one of the UK's top theatrical lecturers in Microbiology, Ben is now a balding middle-aged dad who is trying desperately to claw back some of his youth with a variety of interesting pursuits. He published his first fantasy novel, The Spirit of Things, in 2020 after a creative awakening a couple of years prior. When Ben's not running about after his three amazing kids and lovely Mrs, he tries to best men fifteen years younger in CrossFit competitions for validation. He also plays the drums in an above-average dad rock band and has two Chihuahuas that sleep 22 hours a day.

SILVER WOLVES
(A TALES FROM THE OTHER KINGDOM STORY)

MELISSA WUIDART PHILLIPS

Rolf moved through the forest, seeing the trees now coated in fresh white; brown hands made of twigs reached out, contrasting with the fine latticework of frost that coated them. Rolf was used to travelling alone through the trees, they did not trouble him; he was glad of his thick clothing though, the hat which covered his brown hair, keeping his ears from turning a bright glowing pink. The snow did not coat the ground the way he had heard it used to, no longer a permanent feature of the landscape. But tonight it had returned, lighting his way home with snow-light, that soft, but somehow bright light, that reflected off the snowy landscape.

He thought the landscape Heta had known must once have looked like this. She was half legend now, a story passed around the fire; a girl who had become lost in a great snowstorm, rescued from a frozen lake surface by a watchful spirit, still said to guard travellers who passed along the great lake's shores. Even though the two villages had long since gone, the lake still remained, although it never froze now, even in winter. Rolf suddenly longed to see the lake, the still water. He turned, adjusting the direction of his path; it was a detour, far from the direction his village lay in, but his longing burned too deep to be ignored.

He moved silently, treading softly, barely making any sound as the snow compacted under his feet. Although surrounded by trees, space seemed to radiate around him; it was peaceful, making him feel he could be the only person in the world. Gradually Rolf began to hear a low snuffling sound, the cracking of the occasional twig as something moved through the trees around him. Rolf wondered what it could be; he paused, listening. But there were no other sounds to identify what it might be.

He knew the wolves that used to roam here had long since gone, so it could not be them; but then, what could it be? Wolves were highly respected creatures in the village, powerful creatures who could be both death and guardian. As a young child he had listened in awed silence to the village elders, as they sat around the communal fire, telling the story of the Great White Wolf…

After the Ice Mother had banished Forgiveness, turning her into the first wolf, leaving her to wander the earth forever alone, and after her friends had looked down and wept falling stars of sadness, Forgiveness was seen by another, high above in the vast heavens. The single, silver star looked down; he saw the white wolf and thought her very beautiful. He watched over her through the years, guiding her through the dark with his soft glow.

But one night he longed to be with her so much, that he cast off his heavenly form. The star fell, shooting earthwards, leaving behind his immortal light. When he reached the snowy earth his form was changed; he was no longer of the heavens, but of earth. He too was changed into a wolf, the only trace of his descent from the sky a silver coat, which glowed and shone with light. When the white wolf saw this silver stranger, she greeted him gladly, recognising him as the star that had watched over her for so long. They ran together, playing and rolling in the snow, entranced by each other's company.

But their happiness was not to last for long. The Ice Mother, ever watchful, spied Forgiveness's new companion and was angered by her joy. The Mother of Ice changed the star who had become an argent wolf; changed him into a thousand particles of silver and flung them into the sky, where they stuck, becoming hundreds of new, smaller stars, all lighting up the night with silver. Forgiveness was heartbroken, but the Earth Mother took pity on her, hiding the white wolf away in a cave, where she had two sons and a daughter, with coats as silver as their father's.

The pups were quick and beautiful, possessing magic qualities from their mother. When they were grown, the three wolves roamed free over the earth, protectors of all wolves who were to follow, moving like spirits unseen by most, forever watchful.

Rolf had loved to hear the tale; he had always sat still and quiet, enraptured by it. He wished that he could see the wolves now, here in the forest, even if only a flash of silver coat.

From up ahead, through the trees, the rustling noises of animals came again, catching his attention. Rolf moved slowly, making little sound, creeping closer, wanting not to startle the beast. The trees opened out a little into a natural clearing; the ground was covered in deep snow, tracks crisscrossing around the small space. A family of big wild boar rooted in the exposed brown of plants, hunting for food, making excited snuffling sounds, tusked mouths clearing the snow away from roots. Rolf was upwind of them; his scent had not reached the boars, allowing him a privileged view. He knew the village would usually hunt for food in these woods, he would often join them; but he could not bring himself to disturb these great creatures, it would be wrong on this night of silent snow, when magic roamed free in these woods. Rolf watched the boars for a while longer, thinking of the wolf spirits who would be watching over these creatures in the safety of their forest.

After a while they began to move on, their small swishing tails disappearing off into the trees, leaving nothing behind them but tracks in the snow.

Rolf went on walking then, moving through the trees, heading for the edge where he would come out on the lake shore. The trees began to thin, until he reached their end, stepping out onto the snow-covered open land that ran around the body of water, rising up into hills beyond.

A few lone falling stars drifted down onto the still water, melting on contact. Rolf moved forward, standing just away from the trees' shadow, out of reach of the clumps of snow which fell with a soft thud to the ground every so often; he stood back from the lake, simply happy to look at it from a distance.

As he stood there a figure appeared, coming from the hills to his right, moving towards him through the snow. As it drew closer, he saw that it was a girl, bundled up against the cold, her pale blonde hair framing bright blue eyes and pink cheeks. The girl came over, stopping and standing next to Rolf, her gaze following his out over the water.

"Beautiful, is it not?" she said.

"Yes," he agreed. "I love this place because of a story from when I was young," he added.

"Yes, there are many great tales, this lake has seen many things," said the girl. "What is the story you speak of?"

"It is one from my village," Rolf replied, "about a girl and a spirit."

"Do you know the one about the three wolves?" she asked.

"Yes, the pups of Forgiveness and the star."

"No, the one of Heta and the wolves." She turned to smile at him as he shook his head, eagerness showing in his eyes.

Three seasons had come and gone since Heta had met Tove in the teeth of winter. Now it was spring and the snow was only a thin coating on the ground, reaching just above her ankles. She was once again visiting her sister in the other village. Heta had gone to search for edible plants around the village, scraping at the snow where green poked through, building up the supplies.

She was on the outskirts, in sight of a few huts, safe. Heta bent and scraped the cold snow away from a plant with her stick, then began to pluck the leaves, placing them carefully in a pouch, making sure the leaves did not bruise. She then moved on to another. A cold wind began to blow, lifting strands of her pale hair. She looked up; the spring wind, Wendas, was rare, a biting cold wind that could sweep in fast in springtime, creeping up on the unsuspecting people, cutting like a knife. It lifted the snow, throwing it up in swirls around Heta, quickly obscuring everything from sight as fresh snow began to fall, mingling with the flurries from the ground. She stood quickly, preparing to return to the village.

Then she noticed a dim shape not far from her in the snow. Heta stayed perfectly still, knowing that it must be a wild creature and might be dangerous. It began to move closer, solidifying. It was a she-wolf, but unlike any Heta had ever seen before, with a shimmering silver coat. The piercing yellow eyes stared at her, conveying some kind of message. Then she turned and vanished into the snow. Heta stood frozen, reminded of another wolf she had once met, another one which had not hurt her. This rare silver-coated creature seemed to have no intention of harming her; it fascinated Heta, drawing her to follow it. She took a few steps, knowing that it was unwise, following the unearthly creature anyway.

She moved through the swirling spring snow, seeing no sign of the wolf, but having the sense that it was somewhere close by. Then she heard a human cry from somewhere in the snow.

"Hello?" she called.

"Here," a young girl's voice came back, but from where Heta could not tell. Then she saw the she-wolf again, only for a moment, flicking in and out of sight. Heta moved in that direction, then saw a girl, of about ten, moving towards her; she recognised her as Greta from the village.

"Are you well?" she asked, as the girl reached her and took a firm hold of her hand.

"Yes, but there are wolves here, they followed me," she said, shaking.

"I know,' Heta said, looking warily through the snow, grasping her stick firmly.

"I was looking for svans," Greta explained, "the white sky creatures. They might have stopped at the lake on their way past."

"We need to get back to the village now," Heta said, starting to walk quickly, Greta at her side. Then there was a lull in the wind, the snow dropped away for a moment, revealing three silver wolves closely following them.

"Run," Heta ordered, releasing Greta's hand to grasp the stick with both of her own; the girl did as she was bid, vanishing towards the village.

The silver creatures seemed huge and ominous, Heta

could feel her heartbeat racing as she stared at them. Then the wind blew again, making them vanish from her sight. She heard a single howl ring out, muffled by the snow; then she heard a hoarse voice calling from somewhere near the wolves.

"Zethin, Siguard, Ulva," the woman's voice called, almost too low to be heard; Heta only did because she was so close by.

Then the wind and snow lifted once more.

Heta saw the three silver wolves moving to stand quietly around the figure who had called them, a figure she recognised, before the snow descended again making them all vanish as if they had never been there.

"Tove," Heta smiled, glad to catch a glimpse of her old friend before she vanished into the snow. "I thank you," Heta said; her words were blown into the whiteness, before she turned and followed Greta back to the village.

"I have never heard that tale," Rolf said. "It is wondrous."

"Yes," agreed the girl.

"Thank you for telling it to me," he said.

"You are welcome, but I need to depart now," said the girl, "I have far to walk."

"Yes, I too must return to my village," Rolf agreed.

The girl began to walk away from him, following the shoreline as it curved off, out of his sight. He watched her go, eyes fixed on her retreating form, his thoughts caught up in the story he had just heard. When she had all but vanished, his gaze moved from her, back to the lake. Rolf stared, unable to believe what he saw.

In the few moments he had looked away from it, the surface of the lake had turned to ice; its depths had changed to thick glassiness, smooth and glistening in the starlight. He looked back at the figure, but she had already vanished in the snow-light. Turning to the lake once more, he saw the still waters had returned, the memory of long ago ice leaving with the girl, leaving with Heta.

Time slipped past, the cold of the snow gradually eating through Rolf's clothes, eventually forcing him to stir. He turned back into the wood, slipping beneath the canopy of dark branches, taking the invisible path back to his home, back to the village.

He felt many spirits walked tonight over this ancient landscape; he would be glad to be home now, to be warm in his bed.

Behind Rolf, keeping their distance, unnoticed in the near darkness, slipped three watchful shapes, guarding all who walked in the forest that night. A shaft of moonlight slanted down through the trees, illuminating the shapes only for a moment, illuminating the silver coats of the three wolves.

•

Melissa specialises in fantasy writing, ranging from mythical to urban. She loves reading about different folklore and myths, especially Arthurian, and always has music on when she's writing. She loves nature and the land, especially Wales where she is from originally. She writes both short stories and novels, bringing something different to them with her dyslexia. She's had many short stories read on radio and published in anthologies. She wrote her first proper short story at the age of eighteen, and through serendipity it was promptly broadcast.

She has a short story, Heta's Journey, published in Harvey Duckman Presents… Volume 3, and Shēnghuó's Treasure in the Harvey Pirate Special.

She was also one of the winners of Writing Britain 2015 with her short film script about Aspergic women, 'Unbroken', which was shown at cinema screenings of short films in Hull and Leeds in 2017.

It is now available to view at: https://studio12.org. uk/2020/07/14/unbroken/

FOAM

J. S. COLLYER

I always thought the river smelled like ash. The kids in the fallout unit used to laugh at me for saying so. But it does. I don't know if it's the chemicals or the dried up grass on the banks, but even now, years on, the wind off the water is laden with the scent of something spent and… finished. Burned out. Cold.

I step up to the water line, watching the lace of foam tickle at the pebbles under my toes. The feet still look strange to me… knobbly, unfamiliar and a little blue from the cold. I look at the water and take a moment to wonder what it will feel like, washing against the new skin. I wonder if it will take away the pain.

I should have told him, really. Should have been honest about how much they hurt. Something must have gone wrong when they connected up my nervous system. But I couldn't take away his smile.

"Well, it's been a long journey, Scotia," he had said, "But just look at you now."

His smile always made my insides dance. I smiled in return and I did a little twirl for him, slowly, concentrating on the rolling press of the floor against the balls of my new feet and not the sensation of blades digging into the tender, artificial flesh.

"No pain?"

"No."

"Fantastic. Hop on the bed, then."

Heat rushed through me when his capable fingers checked the scarring around my waist. I held my arms up as instructed as he waved one of his many bleeping machines over the join and asked me to tell him when it hurt and when it was numb.

It was all on fire, but I couldn't bring myself to tell him he'd failed.

"This all looks great, Scotia. The healing is coming along great. Blood vessel connection is good. I think I'm nearly ready to sign you off."

My stomach clenched. "What about my hands, Doctor Olsen?"

Pity tightened his face. "They won't fund it, Scotia. Nothing purely cosmetic. I'm sorry."

I hung my head but after a pause he put his hand over mine. The touch sent jolts through me but seeing his warm, normal hand, skin the colour of fresh bread, resting on my death-pale, stick-like fingers with their extra knuckles, just made everything worse.

"You have beautiful hands."

"They're fallout hands."

"They're unique." He patted them. "No one with natural hands has your level of sensitivity. Someone like me could never paint the things you have, or play the piano the way you do. And now you have real legs, you can take these hands around the world and see what doors they can open for you."

"I just want to be like you."

He didn't say anything for moment but then pulled up a chair and took my deformed hands in both his own. "Scotia, look at me."

I glanced up through my hair and that smile was there again, along with something in his eyes that sent sparks down my spine. I would walk on knives forever to see him look at me like that again.

"You've come so far. So few fallout victims have fought as hard as you. But now look. You can walk, you can swim, run, dance. You have a chance to take yourself wherever you want to go."

"I can dance?"

"Of course." He squeezed my hands. "It'll take a little while to get used to balancing, but give it time and your only limit is your own ambition."

"Will you teach me?"

He laughed then and stood. "I'm not much of a dancer."

"I bet you've done it before, though. That means you're one up on me."

He glanced at the closed consulting room door then held out his hand. I took it, not looking at the way my fingers wrapped too far around his and let him help me up.

"Here," he said, placing my hand on his shoulder whilst

he put one of his own at my waist. It tingled where he pressed my tee shirt against the scarring. He took my other hand in his then started swaying.

"We'll just have to imagine the music," he said. "Now, there, just move your weight from one foot to the other. Careful, now."

I closed my eyes. My blood was singing. My new feet were screaming, but it didn't matter, not with his warmth and the smell of his hair wrapped around me.

"There, see. You're a natural."

A laugh bubbled out of me. We stopped moving. His face was close. My heart thudded against my ribs more than the anti-rejection drugs could account for. Something was burning in his eyes and I felt more complete than even the legs could have made me.

But then he coughed and pulled away.

"No untreated water for another six weeks, remember. Give that skin a chance to strengthen. And I've booked your last follow up with Doctor Holm in three months."

"It's not with you?"

He smiled and looked at me again but he suddenly felt a million miles away. "I'll be a bit busy then, I'm afraid. I'm getting married that week."

I would have walked on knives forever. But instead I take one step then another into the polluted water, feeling the chilly sting against the dissolving flesh. I wonder if it would feel like being ripped apart, or like how they say the acid bombs claw the flesh from your bones. But it's not that bad, not really.

It just feels like I'm melting into foam, merging into the water to become the froth that dances along the pebbles. I realise I like this idea as I step deeper still, stumbling slightly as the river crumbles the synthetic flesh away. Maybe I'll finally feel part of something.

•

J.S. Collyer is a science fiction writer from Lancaster, UK, where she lives with her partner and two cats. She studied Creative Writing to MA level at Lancaster University. Her first novel, Book 1 in the Orbit Series, Zero, a scifi novel described as 'Firefly meets James Bond' was released by Dagda Publishing in 2014 and made it into Northern Soul Magazine's Best Reads of 2014. The sequel, Haven, was released October 2015 and the third and final installment, Silence, was released July 2016. She enjoys writing stories that are larger than life, but with down-to-earth, relatable themes and characters.

Find out more at www.jcollyer.wordpress.com

THE ATAHSAIA IN THE CAVE

PETER JAMES MARTIN

So just to catch you up on what happened last time. We had just done a job in New York City. Sent there by Alice to help out someone she knew. The job involved going deep in the city's sewers so you can imagine the smell we had sticking to us. Anyway, we were expecting a nice express trip back home to Blighty. That was not what we got. What we got was a plane taking us deeper into the USA. Alice wasn't answering any of my calls as to why we weren't going home, with Riz getting worried about people, namely Valarie, snooping around our office the longer we were away from it. Then my phone rang.

"Hello?" I asked, hoping for some answer to what was going on.

"Ah hello, Mr Brennan! No doubt you're confused as to what's going on, and who I am?"

"Der phone sayz yer name is Clyde," Riz piped up, pointing at the caller ID.

"What! How do you know that?" Clyde said, his bravado punctured by technology. What also didn't help for him, was that a while ago, Alice had put a list of important people across the world that I should know, into my phone. These were all contacts of hers. I suppose that was a precursor to this happening, as I quickly got the impression that we were now something that could be loaned to other people.

"What's the deal then?" I said sighing.

There was a cough at the other end of the line, then Clyde continued. "Right, so you know who I am, fine, but do you know why you're not going back home? Or why I have commandeered you?"

"Cuz yer a dick?" Riz was particularly blunt, and while we have lost many an unsavoury client to his behaviour before, here could be more dangerous if we wanted to get home.

"Bigger dick then you, buddy. I mean that in every sense."

Oh great, a pissing contest.

"Hah! In yer dreams twat." I clamped Riz's mouth shut to stop any further vulgar comments or arguments.

"Can you just cut to the chase please?" I pleaded.

"Fine, you want the point, I'll give it to you. Ever heard of an Atahsaia?" I saw Riz's ears pick at the mention of it.

"Aw shit. Der Zuni aren't gunna be happy."

"Well, actually it's not the Zuni who are unhappy. One of the Atahsaia that used to bother them, one got bored, and moved on to new sticks! Boys, you're heading to Arizona! Hope you packed some clothes for the warm weather."

I think he knew we had no belongings with us.

"Arizona! Are you paying for our lodgings?" I demanded to know.

"Alice said I should just take it out of your payment for the job, it's an easy one to do as well, just get rid of the Atahsaia. Simple!" Simple, he called it. What was so simple to getting rid of something that I had no idea about? "Anyway, enjoy the rest of your flight, I'll ring again once you land at Phoenix Mesa Airport." He hung up, leaving us stewing with the details, or the lack of them.

"Well, isn't dis a fine mess."

"Riz, what's a Atahsaia?"

"It's a sort of giant, eats its own kind, or humans. Got long grey hair, tusks, yellow un-blinking eyes, scales on its arms, talons and massive mouths. Yer know der sort of thin."

"Oh, one of those things," I said sarcastically. I often wondered to myself how I got myself stuck in these situations. "Anything else you can tell me?"

"Dey're bastards, like propa twats. Dey try to be tricksters, nd wen dat fails, dey resort ta brute force. Der Zuni were der ones dat normally dealt wit dem. Probs y did one ran away ta sum where dey weren't."

"Sounds like you know the Zuni already. Are they another one of those groups that told you to get lost?"

"Yer cud say dat, I mite ave made a bad impression."

"Gee, wonder how that happened?" Again I was being sarcastic. It's hard to get across like this.

"Don't yer start bein a dick as well," Riz made a point

to turn his back to me, meaning that I wasn't going to get any more out of him till we landed, however long that was going to be. So with nothing but time, I turned to my other source of information, the internet.

Four hours later, we arrived in the Phoenix Mesa airport. Last time, Alice had made special arrangements so I could get through security without alerting everyone to the rat I was carrying with me. I was hoping that we'd get the same treatment. We did not. I was stood on the airstrip, near the plane, for over an hour before someone came up to me, and led me to the fence, where I was advised to 'watch the landing'. This attendant helped me up and then I had to jump from the top of the fence. Who this attendant was, I had no real idea, though it did turn out that this was someone that Clyde had sent to help us. This had solved one problem, but then gave us a completely different one. Where the hell were we supposed to go now? The sun was starting to set, and we had no money, no food and no shelter. Also, we were in fricking Phoenix, Arizona.

"Yer got ne betta at buildin a hut?" Riz asked, knowing full well the response I'd give. I decided not to reply, at least to that comment.

"We just have to wait till Clyde gets in contact, then he'll have something for us to do… And hopefully eat." My phone started ringing, and I eagerly answered it.

"Okay, we're here. Now what?"

"You might want to get out of the way," Clyde replied, backed up by the sound of a mighty engine. One that

I continued to hear even after the call went dead. Two powerful floodlights turned on, blinding me. I couldn't tell much from between my hands, but I guessed this was our ride.

"C'mon boys, get in, just a short ride to Anthem." I stumbled into the car on Clyde's orders, still trying to get my vision back. "I got to tell ya, you weren't what I was expecting," he added.

I guessed he was looking me over. Then Riz popped out.

"Yer know wat dey say bout looks nd dat."

Still couldn't see, but I heard all I needed as Clyde shrieked like a camp movie damsel. If I could have, I would have set it as my message tone. Seems that Alice had neglected to tell him that Riz was a rat. Couldn't help but wonder why she kept that information from him.

"Why do you have a rat in your pocket?" he shouted at me.

"Y do yer scream like a girl?" Riz said.

"Riz be nice," I finally chimed in.

"Wait, that's Riz?" I heard the engine quieten, so guessed that Clyde had slowed down.

"Who were yer expectin? Alice told yer bout me, didn't she?"

"She never said you were a rat. A talking rat at that."

"Kay, long story short, I'm a talkin rat, deal wit it. We got a job ta do, let's jus get on wit it." Riz'd had to explain so many times that he'd got his response memorised for times like this.

"Fine, I'm not anything but professional. Right, first step, take ya both to your motel. Then I got to speak to Alice."

"Yeh, ring'er y she's asleep, great way ta get on her gud side." Riz sniggered. Finally I could see again properly, just in time to see the look in Clyde's eyes, the one of him contemplating dumping Riz out of a car window. If I had a penny for every time I'd been tempted to do that…

"Right, to the motel," Clyde finally said, repeating himself.

Well, I can say that I've stayed in worse dumps. At least the motel Clyde took us to had four walls and a roof, but I've also stayed in far better one star properties. For instance, if you go to book yourself in and the manager is trying catch mice with a fishing rod, you should probably look for somewhere else. Our room was basic, a soft bed, a working TV and an on-suite with that hadn't been cleaned in a month look. So yeah, not the worst if your standards have crashed through rock bottom already. I passed out almost straight away on hitting the bed. I'd no idea what Riz did and I didn't much care to be fair.

Waking up the next morning to a knock on the door, Riz was sat flicking through the channels, complaining like always.

"Yer change countries but dere's still nuthin on!"

Wearily, I grabbed the door, with Clyde on the other side.

"You sleeping beauties ready for this?" he said, as he

handed me the morning paper. One of those sleazy ones where they were just as likely to print some half-baked rubbish as they were the truth. The front page though, offered me my first look at what we were after, an Atahsaia itself. As per usual with stories like this, the photo was blurry, and for those not in the know, blurry enough to dismiss as fake. Just as well really with this creature's reputation. Didn't need anyone else coming out to see it.

"Let me freshen up then," I groaned.

Not long after, we were back in the SUV and driving for Anthem, just north of where we were. Clyde told us a little about the place on the way. It had been what they called a master-planned community, which I took to mean that it had all been planned out from the very beginning. They had an approximately 21,700 people living there, not a number to sniff at, they would all be juicy targets for the Atahsaia. He also bragged about the country club there, praising its bar, which he claimed that he single-handedly had sourced and stocked himself. It was a riveting conversation.

"So wat den, yer want us ta patrol till we find dat thin?" Riz said, sighing.

"Oh no, I'm taking you to where the beast is, in a cave near the country club. As I said, we just want you to get rid of it." Clyde smiled like an idiot, or as someone who only wanted to be thought of as an idiot.

"Kay, makes der job easier, tho if yer already knew where it waz, y not do der damn job yerself!"

I was with Riz on this one.

"Okay, truth time, I had hired a few other guys first before you. They screwed up, and we found their remains on the golf course. Had to tell their families that a black bear got them. Had to think of a story to explain how a black bear managed to get them so far away from the state park."

I think I was supposed to laugh at that story. I didn't.

"Well, yeh, dat sounds like an Atahsaia alrite. Great, yer fed 'im." Riz rolled his eyes, as the car left the road, and roared through the dirt.

"Oh, don't talk like that. I'm sure you can tackle this giant. Should be a piece of cake for the UK's best supernatural exterminators!"

There was a sinister tone there that I didn't like, and not just because I'd never advertised ourselves as anything like that. Generally I advertised as either a private investigator, or a jack of all trades.

"Exterminators?" I questioned, though I never received an answer.

Instead, Clyde excitedly pointed out an opening in the ground ahead of us. "There you go boys, there's the beast's lair. Let's go in! Can't wait to see what you do best. I've brought fireworks just to make sure."

"Fireworks? Hope yer not talkin bout dose pretty thins yer throw in der air," Riz stretched out. "Tho I hope yer did brin sumthin we cud use, cuz we got crap all dat will do much ta a Atahsaia."

In response to Riz's question, I got a pouch throw at me.

"I think these will be all the fireworks we'll need. A special kind of Rune stone that me and the boys have been tinkering with. They'll give you all the boom you'll need and more."

On hearing that, I knew I had to look at what I'd been given. Even without opening the pouch, I knew that what I had was different. The shape was bulkier then what we normally used. They were also a lot heavier. One fell into my hand straight away, and while one side looked the same, I even recognised the symbol as being from my old favourite, the Blast Rune, the other side was anything but. Looking like it had been bashed in, the reverse of the Rune was a piece of crystal, something I recognised from long ago. Etherite, Riz had described it to me before as being a powerful substance, especially to those from the Other. Many a creature had coveted this material. Clyde had been watching my face, as he knew the precise moment to speak up.

"Yup, don't know what you boys are using across the pond, but here, we call these boosted Rune stones. A bit clunky, I know, but I'm not a PR guy. That Etherite will make sure the Runes can take down anything! Regardless of what it is." He seemed really proud of these things. Me and Riz didn't share that, but while I stayed quiet, well, you can guess what Riz did.

"Yeh, dey will take down ne thin, as well as everythin else in der area. Yer ejit! Do yer know wat yer even doin wit dese thins! I'm surprised yer aven't wiped out yer town! Bloody morons."

"Oh please, we know how to use these safely. You won't be sorry for that amount of fire power." Clyde laughed.

"Wait, did those other guys have these? If so, it didn't do them any good," I pointed out, but yet again, I was ignored.

"Right lads, enough chatting, lets get them!" As gung-ho as he could have possibly managed, Clyde jumped out of the SUV, donning a cowboy hat as he did. I got out of the car like a normal person, Riz on my shoulder, and ahead of us, the Atahsaia's lair.

"So we go in then?" I said, rubbing my head. Already the heat was annoying me.

"Yeh, might as well. Didn't feel much like gettin clobbered by a giant but 'ey mite as well get dis ova wit. Jus don't use dose soddin thins. Gettin clobbered is one thin, havin my atom's rearranged by one of dem misfirin is anotha!" Riz shouted, knowing he was in full ear shot of Clyde, who was waving his 'boosted' Runes around like he was playing westerns.

We entered the maw of the cave that had been cut out of the ground, leaving crude marks in the entrance, evidence that it had been hewn with impressive force. We hadn't got very far in before we started hearing unusual sounds.

"What the hell is that?" Clyde shouted, prompting a large shush from me.

The echo of the cave was changing them subtly, but I recognised these 'strange sounds' from sharing a room with Riz for nigh on nineteen years. The giant was snoring. Of course, the further we got in, the less light we had to work with, not that there was much to see. You'd been in one cave of a giant-man eating creature, you'd seen them all. The one thing that seemed to be different that I couldn't check out more, was that it looked like there were drawings on the walls. By the time I discovered it though it'd been too late in taking notice. After everything was said and done, I'd also forgotten I'd seen them in the first place. They're probably still there, waiting for someone to stumble across them and take all the credit for their discovery. I'm not bitter, I swear.

"Riz, I'm going to need you to tell me what's ahead, I can't see anything." I fumbled forward, trying to go in the direction of the noise.

"Oh, lik dat is it? Dat jackass brins der runes of mass destruction, but skimps on der actual thins yer humans need, like soddin torches! Watch out fer der hole," Riz grumbled as I skilfully sidestepped over what I could only assume was a pot hole. Another sound made its presence known, that of dripping water, though thankfully that was never as loud as the snoring. Why am I pointing this out though? Because of what happened next involving our American boss and any element of surprise we could possibly have had.

"Son of a bloody bitch!" Clyde yelled out at the top of his lungs.

My first thought was that something had happened, like we'd been the victims of a stealth attack, or that he'd tripped in a hole. No, it was never allowed to be something like that.

"Wat's wrong, yer smeggin ejit?" Riz growled.

"Water dripped down my back! It was freezing!" Clyde replied, as if it exonerated him.

As if I needed to be told this next part, I could have guessed it.

"Ey Bren, der snorin stopped…" Riz's voice returned to a whisper.

"Oh? You think!" I replied, and my partner turned back to Clyde.

"Yeh, sumthin is comin ta us. Gud job prick."

"Isn't this what we wanted? Now it's coming to get us, we can blast it to the moon and back!"

Clyde did not understand that he'd done something wrong. Clyde is an idiot, don't be like Clyde. I felt a light tremor in the ground, one that was steadily rising. Something heavy was making its way to us. He genuinely didn't see the problem with fighting in this tunnel, with Runes that could go nuclear, to put it mildly. We needed to regroup, but first, we needed a distraction.

"Oi! Twit!" Riz called out to Clyde, who was probably aiming about in the darkness, blindly. "Yer put ne soddin healin Runes in ere?" Riz scurried into my pocket after that 'boosted' Rune pouch.

"Healing? Why the hell would we need that? No one's getting injured, we're going to send this thing to meet its maker!"

I don't think Clyde could have said anything more stupid. Well, he probably could have.

"Stupid ejit! Rite, gotta do dis der 'ard way den!" Riz pulled himself free with one of the Blast Runes in his mouth.

"You going to tell me this plan?" I asked.

"I don't know what you fellas are stressing about, we got this!" Again, Clyde said nothing that was any help.

"Will yer jus shut up! Yer not helpin! As fer der plan? Jus watch me!" Riz used his teeth to ply the glowing Etherite off the Rune, then started chewing at the symbol. By now, the earth was pounding and I heard laughter, getting too close for comfort.

"Who's going to end up in my belly? Who's going to end up in my belly?" The giant said, trying to make it into some kind of chant. Maybe it was Clyde's kindred spirit.

"Not us, yer daft bastard!" Riz shouted as he jammed the Rune in the ground, laughing maniacally as he did. The effect was instant as the cave shuddered, and all the rock that had been thrashed out of the way to make it, reformed quickly creating a solid wall between us and the Atahsaia. Though clearly, Riz hadn't been too careful with cleaning the Rune of all the Etherite as there was a flash as a mix of crimson and jade coloured energy streaks leapt from the new wall and started 'fixing' the rest of the cave.

"Run!" I shouted, trying to be heard over the rumbling as the cave healed itself. Given the new sound of running, I guessed that Clyde had listened to that suggestion and legged it. Riz clung on for dear life as I ran for it as well, though something had caught Riz's eye during this escape attempt, as I heard him mutter all the while.

"Is dat a? Really? Dere's anotha one, nd a soddin notha one! Der walls, he waz puttin dem inta der walls!"

Talk like that is really distracting when you're trying to stay alive as a cave collapses in on you. Ahead of us though was the sweet view of daylight, and I could make out Clyde in front of us, which I guess was a bonus. Riz certainly hates it when the one paying us dies. The rumbling behind me roared even louder. I could tell, without even looking, that the cave was almost fully 'healed' meaning that I was seconds away from a very painful death. Throwing caution to the wind, I jumped out of the exit, and landed with a thud in the dirt.

"Riz, next time, make sure all the Etherite is off," I groaned.

"Quit yer yappin, we made it out, didn't we?" Riz shook the dust off and looked back at where the cave used to be. "Well, dat's der end of dat! Now fer der best part, gettin paid." He smiled as he turned to Clyde who was trying to get his breath back, his hat lost at some point in the chaos.

"Well, boys, that was different! Not what I was expecting, at all. What was the point of giving you those boosted Runes if you weren't going to fire them! One shot, boom." Clyde straightened himself up and then silently mourned his hat.

"Maybe cuz we wanted ta live, yer wazzock!" Riz's mouth remained open like he was going to add to the insulting barrage but no other noise came out. Instead, the look on his face changed, from his sly smirk, to disbelief. "Aw, crap."

"What?" I asked, but I didn't need to have bothered. I felt the ground below me start to rumble violently, like an earthquake that was only affecting us in this tiny area.

"Why is the ground shaking?" Clyde wanted to know, and he was about to find out, as the ground underneath him burst open, a giant's hand reaching out and grabbing him, hoisting him into the air like some sort of ghoulish festival prize. The Atahsaia sounded pleased as punch with what he'd got.

"Look at this! Look at this! Fancy grub!"

From where I was standing, the giant's breath was threatening to peel my skin off. Clyde may have been an idiot, but I did feel sorry for him being so close to the giant's mouth.

"Help! Anyone?" Clyde moaned, fitting his position.

"Oh! Is now a gud time ta use dese 'boosted' Runes?" Riz laughed. It may have sounded out of character for him to laugh at a moment where our client may end up a less then healthy snack, but remember the person we had been dealing with.

"Guys! Help me for Christ's sake!"

I was tempted to join in the teasing, but someone had to step up and sort this.

"Okay, I wouldn't recommend eating him, he's not good for you," I started with a basic line, just to open the dialogue.

"Should I eat you?" the Atahsaia answered back. It was predictable though, and I was prepared.

"No, and I wouldn't recommend eating the rat either."

As I spoke, Riz held up a paw, alerting the Atahsaia to his presence.

"You! You! I know you! Crawling End! You'll taste good."

I wasn't expecting that, but probably should have?

"Surprised yer can taste nethin afta all dat cheap vodka yer been drinkin!" Riz shouted back, which allowed me to piece together what he saw earlier in the cave. This also got me thinking. I didn't have the time to run it past Riz, so I ran with it.

"You like drinking then?"

"Does he like drinkin? Der cave waz littered wit der cheap stuff dat tastes like sumone pissed in salt water!" Riz added.

"I drink what I can get! What I can get! I'll need some more to wash this treat down! Down he'll go!"

I saw Clyde flinch as the Atahsaia breathed all over him.

"Well, how about a drinking competition? You lose, and you don't eat him. Sounds fair right? Plus you'll get to drink better stuff." My plan took everyone by surprise.

"Bren, yer sure bout dis? Yer a stinkin lite weight! I've seen Valarie drink yer under der table. One bottle nd yer'll ave yer undies on yer 'ead doin karaoke!" Riz advised, before I dropped a bombshell on him.

"Riz will be your drinking opponent."

As you may guess, this brought on an instant attitude adjustment.

"Yer wat? Go screw yerself! Y der 'ell wud I put thins at stake fer dat arsehole!"

"You go on the piss with the Norse gods, this should be easy!"

"Yeh, nd all dose times, I'm drinkin Thor's heavenly mead! All yer stuff tastes like socks in comparison!"

"Please, rat! Do it for me! I'm too young to be eaten by a giant!" Clyde pleaded, and somehow made himself more pathetic.

Riz growled.

"Relax," I said, "you'll be fine."

The giant peered at us.

"Me and the Crawling End, drinking? Drinking is fun," the Atahsaia paused, probably mulling over the decision in its head, which I also guessed was fairly empty. Had it been smarter, there was a million ways this encounter could have been far worse. "Yes! I'm in. I'm in to win! But we need drink! No drink left here."

I smiled, with what I was about to say, and while it was naughty, sometimes you could say that Riz has rubbed off on me a bit.

"That's fine, there's a place called a country club over there," I pointed in the general direction of it. "You and Riz can just go and raid its prized selection of booze."

This didn't go down well with the hostage, despite it being his fault I even knew about that place and its 'collection'.

Clyde squealed. "No! Don't do that! Anything but that! I'll lose my membership!"

How cute, he was more bothered about his membership at the club then his own life.

I grinned. "I heard there's a bottle of 52 year old Macallan in there…"

Clyde looked like he was about to have an aneurism.

I stepped up to the giant. "But," I added forcefully, "you do it without hurting anyone. Can't stress that part enough. Then you come back here and get rat-assed."

"Wat 'ave I told yer bout usin dat feckin word!"

"Not now, Riz. I'm busy." I turned back to the Atahsaia. "Well, how about that?" I was pretty proud of my plan. It was relatively risk free, a posh place was going to get trashed, and if things went my way, no one would get hurt. Barring hangovers anyway.

"I'm not agreein ta dis! Yer stupid prick! Yer wanna drinkin contest, yer go ahead. I'm not drinkin dat filth!" Riz pouted.

This caused a laugh from the bowels of the Atahsaia which could curdle blood.

"Crawling End? Crawling to the toilet more like! Can't handle any drink! No drink for him! He sticks to water!" The giant's attempts at taunting ended up working in my favour as Riz's temper flared.

"Rite, dat's it! Yer on yer stupid prick! Not only am I gunna drink yer unda der table, but I'm gunna keep goin till I've drank yer six feet unda! Yer jus watch! Yer may be der size of a house, but I bet yer can't handle der strong stuff!"

"I'll show you how much I can drink! How much can I drink? I drink a valley full!"

"Can I go down yet?" Clyde meekly asked, and in response the Atahsaia smashed him into the ground and then folded the earth over him, pinning him in place.

"You stay here! Here you stay! No running away!"

"Oh god, Brennan! As soon as they've gone, get me the hell out of here!"

It was all going well till he opened his big mouth. The little gears in the Atahsaia's brain must have clicked together as he realised that I would be left alone during this whole endeavour, and that it could all be a ruse so I could save Clyde.

"Need more collateral!" he shouted as he grabbed me and repeated what he done to Clyde, trapping me next to the American. This, sadly, I didn't see coming. Luckily for me, I trusted Riz's ability to drink like breathing air, and win the contest hands down.

"Looky, Bren, yer got yerself a nice hole dere! Waz dis in yer stupid plan too? Great job by der way. Maybe next time yer cud throw in an eating contest or sum otha stupid crap! Guess yer not throwin nethin now, are yer!"

"You're enjoying this now, aren't you?" I sighed, again, knowing the answer already.

"If dis sum how made up fer der fact yer bout ta make me drink a ton of sewage, den yeh."

"Just go get the drink."

"Shall we go den?" Riz asked the Atahsaia who nodded cheerfully.

"Drink! Drink! Drink!" the giant chanted repeatedly.

Riz hopped up to his shoulder, and perched on it, taking in all the extra room he had compared to when he sat on me.

"Dat way!" Riz directed the giant towards the country club. Riz is many things, he's an arsehole, a bastard, but he's also not a cold blooded killer. He likes causing pain, but in a 'I'm going to laugh at you stubbing your toe way' not a 'let's see how many people we kill taking a few bottles' way. I was confident of this even as Clyde next to me was worrying about the damage to both the building and his reputation. My reply was he sounded rich enough to fix both by flashing the cash. With Riz and the Atahsaia gone, this left me with Clyde, and yes, it got boring real quick.

Riz came back within a couple of hours, just as it was getting dark. He bounded up to where I was.

"Miss me? Dat jackass is comin up. We did der old smash nd grab. No one waz dere mind, dey were all on der golf course. Wud luv ta see dere faces wen dey saw wat happened!" Times like this, I do wonder if Riz had other professions in mind.

"And the security cameras?"

"I nibbled der wires, still gunna make der papers, but it'll be one helluva story. Der yank version of der Ministry of Otherworldly Business can 'ave fun wit dat one!"

The Atahsaia came and plonked down the entire bar almost, and started rummaging for the barrels under it.

"We build a fire now! Fire it up! Then drink! Drink

all the drink!" He laughed, which roused Clyde from the sleep he'd fallen into.

"What? Is this madness over with?" He saw the bar in all its glory and promptly passed out again. Just as well, don't think I could have put up with his commentary.

Riz quickly built a fire, using skills I didn't even know he had. Then Riz with a bottle, and the Atahsaia with the barrel, they started drinking. I couldn't tell what the drinks were but it didn't matter as they were gone in a few minutes. This happened a few times. So far none of them seemed any worse for wear. In fact they were laughing at jokes I didn't hear.

"Rum's up next!" Riz called out, rolling a couple of bottles to the giant. "Get dis down yer throat, yer bastard!"

The Atahsaia picked them up, pulled the tops of all of them, then poured them all into his waiting mouth.

"Good stuff! Bring me more! I want more!" the giant roared.

"Oh you'll love wat I've got next! Der expensive vodka!" Riz passed the bottles along, and the giant fumbled them at first, laughing as they slipped around his giant fingers. Once he got them in his grasp, he downed them as well, just like water. In comparison, Riz was steady as a rock, looking disinterested as always.

"Told yer dis stuff waz trash, Bren! It tastes like sweat! Yer ready fer der next drink, I've saved der best fer last" This time, Riz went into the unit that had been ripped out, and came back with two small bottles of a green liquid. I recognised this without needing to be told what it was.

"What? What? What's that then?" The Atahsaia slurred his words, pausing unnecessarily.

"Absinthe," Riz whispered with a devilish grin. He hopped over to the giant and handed him the bottle. The Atahsaia snatched the bottle, after multiple attempts I should add, and then drank it all in one go. He then swayed for a moment, gave out a single laugh, then he fell face forward into the dirt. I saw Riz roll his eyes as he checked the Atahsaia over.

"Daft twat, didn't even ave ta get der turps out, wat a lite weight."

"Well, now that's sorted, how about getting us out of here?" I said, pointing to the earth that covered me like a stony blanket.

"Aw do I 'ave ta?"

"Well, yeah."

"Dat's not a compellin argument! Y shud I?"

"Because any money is paid into my account and you can't access it without me? Plus if Alice found out that you were pretending to be me just to con her. Well, I wouldn't like to be in your paws."

"Shit," Riz scurried over to me, and started Rune crafting again, making a way to get me out. Sadly, to make things worse, Clyde woke up.

"I had the worse dream! That I was stuck in the ground while monsters drank everything!"

"Well dat's a funny thank yer fer savin ma life," Riz rolled his eyes.

Clyde just whimpered to himself.

185

It didn't take long to get us freed, and as Clyde mourned for his deceased bar, I had to organise for the Atahsaia to be taken back to Zuni territory, where he belonged. Luckily, the people I managed to find, looking through the expanded contacts on my phone, arrived quite quickly. As the three of us watched the giant being taken away by the largest big rig I'd ever seen, under a thick cover, of course, I asked the only question that mattered.

"Can we go home now?"

"Oh no, there's still more to do," Clyde sniffed. "A lot more to repay for my lost bar."

"Fantastic," I groaned, longing for my bed.

"Not like it can get ne worse, Bren," Riz said.

Oh, if he only knew.

•

Peter James Martin is an author who knows a thing or two about talking rats, namely that they'd make terrible pets. Nestled in the North East of England, on the banks of the River Tees, he lives with his family and two Shih Tzus. Want more of Brennan and Riz? Then follow him on Twitter at @Brennan_and_Riz where he posts mini adventures of the duo through the #vss365 tag. There's also short stories and Folklore galore over at his blog: https:// tstpjm.blogspot.com/

The Strange Tales of Brennan and Riz are available in paperback and in e-Book, and Peter's first novel, Brennan and Riz: A Boy and a Rat, is due out in 2021.

SPLINTER OF HOPE

C. K. ROEBUCK

Flashes in the night sky, explosions soon followed, and little by little the planets were turned to dust.

The war raged on year after year, and with each year that passed the war turned more brutal, more destructive. The dead outnumbered the living and Tor-Gar could see that extinction was inevitable for both of the warring worlds in this solar system. With no hope in sight he fell into depression.

He left for work each and every morning, numb like some drone running on automatic, leaving without a word, like some undead thing his wife barely recognised. Tor-Gar's wife Tor-Soo did not know the details of her husband's work, all she knew was that in contrast to her own profession as a computer programmer, he was a biological scientist and that the company he worked for had been acquired by the Establishment some time ago. It had come as a surprise to Soo then when half a Luna cycle ago Gar returned home from work one evening mumbling to himself, seeming excited in one moment then in the next angry and cursing, clearly in disagreement with something or someone. From that moment everything changed.

Gar had gone to work that day as usual, like every other day and like every other day he couldn't remember getting there. He hated his life and his work, especially his work. He knew that most likely anything discovered or created in this lab would be taken by the Establishment and be perverted to serve the war, and for some reason, a reason unknown, there were three Agents of the Establishment in his lab, two males and a female awaiting him. Gar knew immediately that they were Agents by the clothes they wore, the plain grey suits that only Agents wore. Gar started to sweat. He wanted to tell them to leave but as his lab was now owned by the Establishment he dared not. It would mean his end of employment, and he and his wife would be as good as dead. No one could be unemployed, anyone on this world without work would be forced into hard labour in the mines or worse. That was not a fate he would have befall himself nor his beloved Soo. The house of Tor would not fall as a result of him being unable to hold his tongue.

As Gar entered through the thick glass door to his lab, he felt all the colour drain from his face as the three Agents turned as one to face him.

"Good day, Tor-Gar, so pleasant to make your acquaintance," the foremost of the three said. "I am Gre-Lor. We are representatives of the Establishment," he announced, holding out his left hand as was the custom.

"Good day, Gre-Lor. I am pleased to greet you and your fellow representatives," Tor-Gar returned the hand gesture as was also the custom. Trying his best to appear pleasant, Gar bowed low, and while keeping his legs straight and together, he kissed the red stoned ring that Gre-Lor wore on his left hand. It took everything Gar had not to show any hostility, not even an errant bad thought towards Gre-Lor. He had to keep up this charade of pleasantness so he performed as was expected of him. He held the kiss for just a second then released the Agent's hand and stood straight once again.

"I am but a humble servant, sir. How may I be of service?" Gar asked.

The lead Agent held out a memory crystal for him to take. Gar took the stick and dipped his head in thanks. "May I enquire, sir, for what purpose am I to use this data?" Gar had to be very careful. Agents of the Establishment were not known for their pleasantness, nor their mercy should a subject not adhere appropriately to protocol. The fact that there were three Agents here suggested the great seriousness of this meeting. It was known that when three Agents appear in unison that one was the Messenger and the other two were Witnesses. The Witnesses had perfect memory and even though they had technology at their disposal to record such meetings, the technology didn't instil such fear as could be achieved by the presence of the two Witnesses. It was long rumoured that all Witnesses possessed telepathy and Gar could well believe it. As he looked at them, he could practically feel their stares penetrating his skull.

"Gar, it seems that the Establishment requires your skillset," the Agent said, drawing his attention. "You are proficient in bio-engineering are you not?"

Gar knew that was a statement, not a question. He had no doubt that the Agent knew every detail of his education so he simply nodded in confirmation.

"We understand that the subject of your educational thesis was on the theory of an organic bio-assembler. On that device are the requirements for what the Establishment requires you to build."

Gar looked at him, stunned. His thesis was just that, a theory nothing more. How was he supposed to create a microscopic creature from scratch, one that could theoretically reorganise other biological matter? Gar just didn't have the equipment to make such a thing.

As though his thoughts were indeed being read, the three Agents blinked in unison then Lor nodded as if some silent agreement had been made.

"Your new bio-manufacturer is being brought in as we speak," the Agent stated, the corner of his mouth curling into a sneer.

All Gar could do was convey to the Agents his compliance and hope that they would leave before his fear gave way to some stray thought that could in all possibility end his life.

"Your humble servant thanks you for your offer to allow him to prove his worth to the Establishment," Gar said, the phrase that all citizens had learned as children. "Is there any other function I may perform before you take your leave?" he asked the Messenger like the good citizen he pretended to be.

"That is all. Everything you need to know is contained

on that crystal," said the Agent. "The Establishment requires your work to be completed in one Luna cycle. Good day."

On those final words, the Agents filed out of the lab, leaving Gar speechless.

How was he supposed to do this in one Luna cycle? Gar knew when he wrote his thesis all those years ago that the possibilities would be endless. In the right hands such a creature could end world hunger, end disease. But in the wrong hands it could unmake any or all life at the whim of its creator.

He inserted the data crystal into his computer and looked on as the screen image, the once serene beauty of his favourite lakeside retreat was replaced by instructions to build a weapon with one purpose only, to destroy life.

Gar at first felt great anger at this order. He knew in his heart that he could never create such an abomination. But what if he could perform another purpose with this creation? He asked himself, what if he could create instead of destroy? He was roused from his thoughts by the bang of the lab door crashing open. Two young men he had never seen before nodded a silent greeting before wheeling in the device that was to become his focus for the coming month. Such a marvel it was, a technological marvel that could create biological structures from carbon, silicone or a combination of the two. Though to Gar's knowledge the latter had never been done, until now at least.

Gar arrived home that day and his mind unlike previous days was alive with thoughts and ideas. He didn't even realise he was mumbling until he felt his wife place her hand on his shoulder.

"Gar, I have not seen you this animated since…" She paused. "I have not seen you like this for a very long time. What has happened?"

Gar explained what had happened at work and even though he knew that he could trust his wife with is life, he dared not tell her his plan yet. Soo looked at him suspiciously and he knew that she could tell he wasn't telling her everything.

"I trust and I love you, my husband. Whatever you are up to, please promise me that you will be careful," she said seriously then she stood back and smiled. "It's good to have you back, my love."

Gar stood there for a moment confused. Where had he been?

Day after day he went to work and continued as ordered. At one point he even retrieved his original notes from his education file as he couldn't for the life of him remember the design of the mechanism that the creature would require to allow self-hibernation. Eventually the creature, or in actuality creatures, began to take shape. Two designs Gar created, one of them to the specifications of the Establishment with a minor alteration, whilst the other he created to resist all manner of adversities. The creature that Gar created for his own purpose could replicate, withstand intense cold, heat, dehydration, radiation and even the vacuum of space. The creature that he created for the Establishment was exactly as the requested data specified, almost identical to his own design but it was limited in its lifespan and replication cycles. That meant that the creatures used for war would be limited in the destruction they could cause. Gar hoped that this would buy him the time that he needed to complete his project. He knew that his race, like that of his neighbouring planet was doomed. He had heard rumour of a new weapon being built, a weapon that could actually control the star that gave them light and life. This new weapon would be even more deadly than the energy bombs already being tested by both planets. With these weapons of such destruction, he knew mutual annihilation was inevitable.

Gar had to be extra careful now. He had an idea but to succeed he had to be bold. More importantly, he had to make sure he did not get caught.

Now half a Luna cycle later, Gar came home from work, this time with a purpose. He opened a large carry case and took out strange containers as his wife stood and watched. Gar stood still suddenly, coming to a decision. He looked straight at her.

"My darling wife. I have something I have to tell you and it is very important." I must do this, he thought, I have no other choice. Then Gar laid out his plan, and told his wife all he had discovered and that it would ultimately destroy them all.

The news at first caused panic in Soo. "Go to the council," she said. "What do you hope to accomplish with all this?" She knew as she said the words that it would make no difference. If it was discovered that they did not agree with any aspect of the war, they would both be labelled traitors, their fate would be sealed, and death would soon follow.

"Soo, I cannot do this without you. Please help me do this or all is lost," he pleaded.

She closed her eyes and took a deep breath. She looked at her husband, the man that she swore an oath to love and honour until death takes them. "What do you need me to do, my love," she said.

"Simple, my love. I need you to steal a weapon satellite," he replied.

Soo laughed so hard, Gar could not remember the last time he heard her laugh so. She stopped abruptly and looked at Gar. Her husband was dead serious. He was not laughing.

Soo was quite an adept computer programmer. What Gar needed her to do was the exact opposite of what she usually did, writing computer programs to stop others hacking into them. Gar needed his wife to hack into their new weapon satellite.

Gar already had several million of the microscopic creatures created and stored safely, but that now seemed like it was the easy part. He needed three more things, a suitable destination, a suitable asteroid and a way to get his creatures to the asteroid. A destination he had found quickly, a little under 12 light years away, another yellow star with several planets in orbit and one of the planets was ideal. It already supported primitive life and it had the right atmosphere. The only problem that he could see was that the star had some unusual radiation spikes and solar flare activity that could destroy mammalian life. That was where reprogramming of the weapon satellite came into play. All he needed now was to find an asteroid and a way to get the samples to it. One problem at a time, Gar, he told himself as he felt the excitement of success build up inside him. The end of the Luna cycle would soon draw to an end and already Gar had started to receive messages requesting updates on the progress of the project. He dared not tell the Agents the work that they had requested was already complete for he feared what would happen should his duplicity be discovered, before his own plans were made final.

As the day drew closer, Gar started to feel like he was losing. Neither he nor his wife had come up with a plan to transport the samples of his creatures to a suitable asteroid. He was beginning to feel an impending doom, a feeling that was exaggerated by the sensation that he was constantly being watched. He found himself scared of every shadow as he made his way home from work. So paranoid was he that he almost turned around and walked away that day he arrived home to find the window coverings closed. The window coverings were never closed before he arrived home from work. As Gar walked the path to his home's front door, he felt his heart pounding against the inside of his chest, his breath held tight as he took his last few steps towards the door. As Gar slowly opened the door, he heard the voices of two females. One of them belonged to his wife but the other, he did not know.

"Gar, wait!" Soo shouted as she rushed over to block Gar before he could enter the house. But Soo was not fast enough. Gar had already caught sight of the female guest in their home. He froze there, standing in the doorway as his wife pulled him inside so she could close the door. No one could know of their guest or all would be lost. There would be no lie they could tell that would not be discovered, no way to explain why this Witness, one of the two that had accompanied the Messenger, Gre-Lor to his lab, was in their home.

"Gar, my love, this is not as it seems," Soo told him. "We are not in trouble, Gar." She took hold of her husband by the shoulders and guided his terrified trembling body toward a seat. He sat as though oblivious to her interaction, all the while staring at the Witness. "Gar, this is Hun-Jay and she is here to help us."

On those words Gar blinked and looked to his wife. "Help us?" he said. "What do you mean, my wife? Here to help us." Every word he uttered trembled with fear. He felt a great need to fly, to get as far away as he possibly could, but he simply could not move, frozen with fear as he was.

"Tor-Gar, I am not here to harm you or your wife,"

the Witness said. He heard the words of the witness yet he did not see her lips move. "I know of your plan and I wish to help you." The female named Hun-Jay nodded towards him and smiled, a warming smile.

"My husband, the Witness knows everything. It was Jay that leaked the existence of the weapon satellite. She will not betray us," said Soo, trying her best to placate her husband.

"I assure you, Gar, that if my intent was to cause you harm, I would have done so already," Jay said aloud. "Please listen carefully, my time is short so I must be brief."

Gar realised that his options were limited. He had no choice but to listen to this Witness Hun-Jay and so he let out a tense sigh and nodded.

"I will listen to what you have to say, Witness. It seems that I have little choice," he said. "I must know one thing, have you been following me these last few days?"

"You are perceptive, Gar," she replied, dipping her head in regret. "For that I must apologise. Please understand, Gar, I had to be sure that I could trust you. The Establishment has spies everywhere and many of my people have been betrayed by those that we believed could be trusted."

"Your people?" asked Gar, wondering what she meant by that.

"Yes, Gar, you should know that you and I are not alone. There are many more like us that do not agree with the philosophy of the Establishment." She paused and took a breath. "I am part of a rebellion, a group of dissidents if you will, but there are just too few of us to make a difference. We are fighting an uphill battle that we will most definitely lose."

"So what do you need from us?" said Gar. He turned to look at his wife and turned back to the Witness. "Why are you here?" he asked.

"Gar, I am here because I believe that the peace we so desperately long for, the end to all the death and destruction, will only come when we are all dead and there is no one left to fight," said Jay emphatically as tears streamed down her face.

"Here, please use this," said Soo as she handed a tissue to the Witness.

Jay took the offered tissue and wiped her face. She paused a moment to compose herself. "Thank you," she said and managed a smile. "You asked why I am here," she stated. "I am here because my friends and I believe that your plan is the only way. We know that we will all be gone long before the new world is seeded of our kind. We will never see the children of your creation return. However, my friends and I are able to help you complete your project." Jay reached her hand into her pocket and pulled out a data crystal. "Here take it," she said to Gar.

Gar reached over and took the offered crystal. "What is this?" he asked.

"Some of my friends work as miners," she said. "These friends mine the asteroids that lay in the belt between our world Orbis and our so called enemy, Patraim." She pointed at the data crystal. "On that crystal is the location of an asteroid that we believe is best suited to your needs. It is of significant size and has already been harvested of all its heavy metals."

"Please excuse my ignorance, but how are we to get the creatures onto this asteroid if all the mining has already been done?" Gar asked, feeling confused.

"Fortunately for us, another journey to the asteroid is required to retrieve the last of the mining equipment. I only ask that you entrust your creatures to me and I will see to it that they are deposited onto the asteroid," she replied.

Gar saw one problem with this, one piece of the puzzle that had not been set into place. He looked to his wife, about to ask her how much time she needed to complete her part of the plan.

"I know what you are to ask, my love," Soo told Gar, smiling. "The task that you set me, I have already completed this day. I need only add the destinations of the asteroid and the new world and then broadcast the data."

They all agreed on this plan, Gar gave Jay the creatures that he had created and so all was set into motion and at last, he felt a splinter of hope, maybe not for his people but for a future incarnation of his kind.

Two days later a lonely asteroid saw the departure of the last of the miners that had taken all they could from it, but it was left with a small gift, a gift that would endure for millennia before finally serving its final purpose.

Shortly afterwards, a satellite that was intended as a weapon received a message, a message that told it to go on a very long journey, though first it must give a lonely asteroid a nudge. The asteroid and the satellite would partake the same journey for the most part and though they would one day, in the far distant future enter the same star system, they would land on very different worlds. One would destroy then create, but the other, the one meant as a weapon, would watch from a distance and protect until the time came for the children to return home.

•

Craig is an electronic engineer, originally from Barnsley and has lived in County Durham for over twenty years. Craig has been an avid scifi fan since watching Blake's Seven as a child, and since then he has loved both watching and reading scifi. Splinter of Hope is his debut as an author. He is currently working on his first full length scifi novel, Sleep, set in the not too distant future where the main character has subjected himself to an experiment that goes a bit wonko. Find out more at cragy.org.uk/wp and follow on Twitter @CKRoebuck

THE BOY IN THE GIANT
(A TALE OF THE WOODS)

JOSEPH CARRABIS

Once upon a time, when a small, magical child lived in a magical woods, a horrible thing happened. Someone left the child outside in the cold, rainy, wet damp of dawn. It doesn't matter if this happened once or a thousand times. When you are a child, even once is enough.

It so happened, as the child grew into a boy, that others came by who were blind to the child and the boy, and splattered mud as they passed. The mud covered the growing boy, its coldness reminding him of being abandoned in the cold, damp dawn.

The child grew into a clever boy. He kept his eyes open and watched the flowers spreading their petals to let in the morning sun, spiders spinning delicate webs stronger than the strongest steel, and squirrels and ants busying themselves gathering winter's harvest.

Over time the boy fell in love with the world around him and decided that no matter what happened to him, he could learn from it. Quickly the boy's wisdom grew as he watched and studied and quietly observed until he became quieter and wiser than most in the Woods.

But while he grew, there was a mud caked child inside, a child the wise boy knew nothing of, crying in the cold, damp dawn. The boy lived with the ache of the child inside so long he thought the pain normal, a part of life, something simply there, constant and forgettable.

The boy sat and watched the mud cake around him as others splashed, and noticed it hardened as it dried. The child gave the boy an idea.

"What would happen if I took some mud and fashioned a cloak around myself?" As the mud hardened he could make the cloak stronger and harder. Eventually the cloak would keep out the cold and the rain and protect the boy and child from pain.

The boy grew into a man who grew on the cleverness of the boy. The cloak became more and more a wall, growing thicker and more impenetrable over the years, eventually giving the man the look and feel of a giant. The man learned to move the giant-like cloak without harm. Sometimes the man would do things that cracked the shell. Then the small child within, remembering the damp and cold, would find more mud to reinforce his prison.

For that is what the giantish wall, the cloak which looked like a giant, truly was. It protected the man who was once a boy and would always be a child, but few could see the child hidden deep within.

And occasionally, every so often and in the quietest

of times, the frightened child would peer out from the giant's eyes in wonder at the Woods.

One day the child did this and saw a small white bird perched on a tree. The giant sat and watched the small white bird. 'How beautiful,' thought the child and boy and man. 'To be so delicate and as graceful.' Just as he thought these things, the bird looked at him and beat its wings until dust clouds rose from the ground. Then it took to the air and began flying directly at the giant.

The child was worried the bird would be crushed when it struck the giant face. The man tried to move away but wasn't fast enough. The little bird flew directly towards him and, just as the boy thought it would die, it crashed through the hard face the man wore.

It flew down, faster and faster, down the caverns and darkness inside the giant, past the fears and sorrows the man had gathered over the years, past the rills and rents others had given the giant not knowing of the boy, deeper and deeper down to where the magical child lay.

"Do you want walls around you forever?" the small white bird asked.

The small white bird spread its wings. It gathered the light coming in high above through the giant face and began to spin. It stayed in one spot, hovering over the child, huddled and frightened beneath the light as it shined and dripped from the little bird's wings. The light splashed the walls of the child's giantish prison. The child looked at the light and realised it was a fire of joy and sorrow which splattered the walls around him. The walls steamed and cracked and began to chip away.

The little bird burst into flame and grew in size as the fire of joy and sorrow boiled the prison walls. The flames lit up the child, boy, and man. At the heart of the flames, in the core of the fires, was a great Eagle, an Eagle with the magical child's face, spinning as did the little bird before it.

The man, more frightened than ever before, stayed huddled underneath the flames. The boy, more curious than afraid, watched the flames melt away the giantish walls. It was the child, remembering the cold, damp dawn, who felt the warmth of the Eagle's fire and stood up underneath, straight and tall, straighter and taller than he ever had before. As he breathed, the fires of joy and sorrow rushed through him, doing to him what they had been done to the walls around him.

The child grew. In odd and strange ways, he grew.

The magical child got taller and stronger. The boy stood up and the child felt himself move into the young boy's body. Next stood the man, and the magical child in the boy walked into the man as well. For the first time, the child knew who he was and felt both the boy and the man with him.

"How can a child grow thus?" He thought it must be the Eagle, spinning and churning, pulling his body and making it grow.

The Eagle flew higher and faster, a blazing tornado pulling the child up through the layers of the giant. On the outside the giantish shell grew hot and red and began to crack and splinter. Just as the Eagle flew through the opening, the giantish form exploded.

The child looked around him. Pieces and fragments of the walls he'd made lay all around him, some smoking, most scattered and turning to dust. The Eagle was still before him. "Look around you, small one."

The child did but it seemed he still looked through giant's eyes. "What have you done to me?"

"Nothing, little one. All you see around you, you have done yourself."

"How could I? All that I created to protect myself is destroyed, but I still see through giant's eyes."

"But now they are your eyes. Your eyes are now seeing your truth. Only those who are truly free can see their own truth. When you see who you are, you see all others as they are. Your freedom is your truth. It is knowing your truth that sets you free. There is no cloak, no wall, no giant other than the giant you are."

The child looked at his arms and legs. He was indeed a giant, far more a giant than the mud caked walls and cloak he'd always thought to be.

"All the wounds you protected yourself from, all the pains you buried deep within those walls, share now. Share them with me and others in and out of the Woods. It is time, awake, you have a song to sing." The Eagle flew up into the sky.

The child felt wings of fire grow from his back, and, spreading them skyward, followed.

Joseph Carrabis's short fiction has been recommended for the Nebula (Cymodoce, May '95 Tomorrow Magazine) and nominated for the Pushcart (The Weight, Nov '95 The Granite Review). His work has recently appeared in Across the Margin, The New Accelerator, Allegory, parAbnormal, serialized in The Piker Press, HDP, podcasted on Chronosphere Science Fiction, Daikaijuzine, and the Write Festival's Fantastic Stories Anthology. His first indie novel, The Augmented Man, is getting 4 and 5 star reviews on Amazon, Goodreads, Barnes&Noble, and others. His two self-pubbed books, Empty Sky and Tales Told 'Round Celestial Campfires, are getting 5 star reviews (and he has more books in the works). Joseph holds patents covering mathematics, anthropology, neuroscience, and linguistics. When not writing, he spends time loving his wife, playing with his dog and cat, flying kites bigger than most cars, cooking for friends and family, playing and listening to music, and studying anything and everything he believes will help his writing.

Find out more at https://josephcarrabis.com

PITSTOP

ALEXANDRINA BRANT

It was difficult to tell which had suffered more: the spacecraft or the fuel station around it.

Coughing into her elbow, Molly stumbled out of the craft. The vehicle had that smell about it that you got in mechanisms past their prime – a rubbery, last week's oil smell. It hadn't been new for years, judging by the scratches on the faded ceiling and the chairs throwing up their stuffing, patched with tape and a sonic blaster's repair function. A zombie spacecraft.

Trust one of the exhausts to blow as they'd wobbled through the fuel station's atmospheric shell, too.

So far, the craft was winning for damage accrued, but the building – a hangar? – they'd 'parked' in came a close second. The grating, a criss-cross of iron, had been warped by the craft's hull and they'd left scorch-marks on the bay doors.

"Geez," Molly called behind her. "When you said we'd make it to refuelling, Nix, I thought you meant we'd make it without falling apart."

Predictably, when Phoenix stuck her dark head out of the door, it was already marked by ash, a thumbprint smudge like a birthmark over her cheek. She'd shoved on her glasses, tortoiseshell square frames that only widened grey eyes – which meant that she had an idea. A mechanical, sciencey idea.

Or half of one. Or was pretending she had one and was trying to grasp it from thin air.

"Huh? Hold on… just need to check…"

She retreated into the craft to the sounds of a rubber hammer hitting the console, much that that would actually achieve, followed by the blare of a fire extinguisher like those metal canisters you found on Earth that had sprayed foam before scientists had found a way to contain flames between holographic meshes.

The cacophony finished with a sharp word in Nix's own tongue – the translator-pod in Molly's ear didn't bother. Which usually meant someone was cursing their head off.

Probably appropriate seeing as their ride out of the galactic vector had given up.

Nix's head popped out of the craft door, all bright eyes and channelling Bambi if Bambi had a backbone to chase the hunter. She shot Molly a grin and switched back to Neutral Earth English.

"Yup. The dorsal engine's shot. Shame. I thought I did a good job with that. Well, a good enough job to get us a bit further…"

Then she cleared up the downwards slant of her eyebrows into something far prettier. Rubbing her cuff against the mark on her cheek – making the mark bigger and giving her white shirtsleeve a nice grey stain – she bounced out of the craft.

"Hello?" Her voice echoed around the hangar even though the room extended the equivalent of the Royal Albert Hall. "No one's home."

"I can see that."

Space-authorised flying vessel after flying vessel occupied the building – maybe fifty, maybe more. Some were the size of an autodrive like the one Nix had built, room enough for a pilot and a mechanic and a cat if you were the type of person who thought it sensible to bring cats into space. Anyway, some of the crafts were not the size of an autodrive. Some of them were much, much bigger.

Some of them outstripped even the Aurora-brand cruisers.

"Oy. Stop gawking, waitress, and give me a hand."

Of course, nothing dazzled Nix. A pink unicorn with sparkles for eyes could've landed and called itself a craft and Nix wouldn't have cheered at the mechanic's ingenuity.

Instead, the woman tossed back her coat, rolled up her sleeves and vaulted against the nearest craft's slanted side-wings. She leaned against the pilot-side door. Even with her glasses stored in her top pocket, her eyes glinted, full and warm.

Oh no. Dodging the craft's landing-wheels that protruded rudely from its body, Molly said in her own crude way to distract Phoenix from her favourite hobby,

"So, funnily enough, I've never used a refuel station before." Pleasure star-cruisers had onboard mechanics and picked up fuel every planetfall. "Aren't there supposed to be… attendants or… something?"

People who tended to stop kleptomaniacs from ripping the doors off other beings' vehicles.

"Phoenix. What are you doing?"

"Tools."

"What?"

"Do you have them? All I need is a wrench, a sonic probe, *anything* to get this door open. The station? Used to be a moon. Like Jupiter's but less… smoggy. One of the Bindetti Companies bought ownership to it in…" Nix squinted one eye as she thought. "Think it was 2243. *Yes.* Same year as the NeoRomanic-Stellar wars. Which meant they lost it – in a poker battle, one of my favourite historical events, I'll have you know, shortly afterwards. Which means it was… let's say won, by the H'katc'I Family, who converted the surface to what you see before you."

"Decent grasp of history. Always corporations," Molly pointed out. She added, "Don't you have–?"

"–a vendetta against corporations? Nope. I just would rather they leave civilisations be."

"I was going to say a screwdriver."

"Oh. That, too." A quick pat of her pockets. "Wait. Hang on. No – I don't. The blaster…" Her eyes trailed towards the back end of her craft; in response, the right exhaust, the one that had so prominently reminded Molly of her impending doom on their descent, expelled a plume of acrid black smoke.

"The blaster's in the back of the craft, isn't it?"

"On the bright side – it's not on fire anymore."

Molly laughed. She couldn't believe it – she actually laughed. God, it had been a long week: the running, the hiding, the arguing her way out of being enslaved… Her laughter echoed mockingly and she filed the memories under *things to haunt Molly when she can't sleep.*

"Odd, though," mused Nix. She sprang back from the door and landed on her feet artfully. "This silence. Fuel station like this should be heaving with beings. Mechanics, pilots, passengers. Even – get this – oxygen waiters. Imagine that? A waiter serving oxygen for *spacecraft*. You and I, we need it to breathe; other species are born bio-cybernetic and they breathe oxygen oil. That's why I. Love. These places." She paused, as if to calm down her pitch, which had been steadily climbing. "*Anyway*. That's why they chose a moon, see – no day, no night. Say what I will about the businesses in *Ignis Constella*, but that's actually acumen. Any time a craft needs refuelling… the station's open."

Except now. When it was very clearly – *shut.*

Wait. Did Nix just say that a species existed that had organic and cybernetic body parts? No – Molly shook her head. She'd dwell on those implications later.

"But if it's meant to be their equivalent of my 24-7," she started, "is there, like, an office or something?"

"Office. Yes. Good thinking." Nix patted her on

the shoulder than rolled onto her tiptoes, managing to bounce ahead without looking as if she'd moved a foot at all. "Like a little office. People to talk to."

Molly trotted after Nix. The hangar wasn't difficult to navigate, if you took out all of the crafts that someone had parked without logic or sense. A glass ceiling poured down light the blue of cuckoos' eggs to keep them from tripping over the tubes that ran from craft to craft and from the mechanisms to orifices in the walls.

"Should be at the back of the station. Tends to be," Nix called. "Oh." Her blue-tinted lips formed a beautiful, round circle, and pursed into place for long enough that Molly had to raise an eyebrow as a question.

To answer it, Nix glanced upwards.

It punctured the light, the pillar of titanium. Two more positioned behind it made the machine a tripod and the two in front of Nix made it some kind of… penta-pod. An oblong body loomed between them, sleek until tips of glass and steel poked out from underneath like two hideous teats. Teats of death that spat something far worse than milk.

"Phoenix?" Molly slipped a hand onto her shoulder. An attempt at a comfort she already knew she couldn't bring. "It's not one of theirs, is it?"

Her lips drew into a thin line. The movement pushed her hair from her cheeks. Her shoulders stiffened.

Then she zoomed across the room, dodging two pillars, making towards where the hangar wall pinched into an inner doorway.

"I'm thinking best if we pay the office a visit first, explain the situation and all that, and then we get ourselves back here pronto – together, naturally – hotwire the first craft we see with its keys still in the ignition. You love autodrive analogies. Here's some more: we keep driving 'til we hit the next refuel station, then the next. Don't stop 'til our ride's only got an inch of juice."

Molly navigated around a pillar. If she held hands with three clones of herself, she'd circle its base. Damn it – it had so many hatches and storages that, as much as she hated the thought of hanging around it, she kept her eyes trained on it.

She started, "I'm just thinking, y'know, The Militaria won't be on your back for much longer, so you don't have to keep zooming around. I know it's silly of me to think that I can change anything, and, don't get me wrong, I'm not asking to go back to the slow path around the galaxy, but you don't have keep pushing yourself from one planet to another. And maybe we can settle for something in the middle. You know? Phoenix?"

Molly glanced at the figure ahead of her.

Nix wasn't there.

For worlds' sake!

"I was talking to you!" she yelled at the ends of the trenchcoat as it slipped behind a glass-topped vehicle that looked as if it belonged not in the stars but on the water.

"You were?" Nix's head appeared. She scratched the back of her neck. "Sorry... I... Nahh."

Yet another behavioural quirk to file under *bits of Nix that would need more analysis later.*

213

"Wot'cha."

Nix raised a hand. Something between her finger and thumb glistened. The scales across her nose and cheeks glimmered in an amber light Molly traced from a dying bulb inside the craft. Someone had left their lights on, left it open for scavengers, jewellery to a thief.

"No. We are not doing this again. Put. The gemstone. Down."

Nix exhaled. Her whole body sagged, readying to argue.

"You!" yelled a voice from across the station floor.

Nix! Molly sprinted to the craft and pulled her away. Actually… you didn't just pull Nix. For starters, she had a density greater than a human all packed away into that tiny, tidy and extra tall frame of hers. And then there was the fact that Nix wouldn't be pulled – not that way anyway – she had too much gravitas of personality.

As if 'gravitas' made any difference against the being striding across the grating. If Nix was 70% legs and arms, then this being was the full 90%, stretched and sweeping and grey. And foreboding. Charge-them-with-criminal-intent foreboding.

A pulse of air shoved her shoulder and decimated the side-wing Nix had been perching on.

Carrying-weapons-level foreboding, too.

Her hand slipped into Nix's and they ran.

"Left!"

Their bodies slammed into each other as they took the corner at different running speeds, and heat surged through Molly's. She wasn't used to this. Not the running – Molly had her silver medal for the Camden under-sixteens running club championship pinned to the kitchen board at her mother's flat back home.

Just… this. Having someone look at her the way she looked at them, all excitement and burning stars and universes to save.

Left, as Nix dictated, took them under another star-craft towards the back of the hangar. Here, the ceiling no longer welcomed in the blue planet-light and instead presented a shaft of dark, glossy rock obscuring the moon's landscape beyond it.

"I… hate you," Molly said as she caught her breath. Her vision bloomed with a mismatch of stars – not the spacey kind, the *blink-and-you're-unconscious* kind.

"No, you don't." Nix grinned.

"You realise he was only yelling at us because you were breaking. Into. His vehicle!"

"Maybe. More fun that way."

"Stop. Stealing. People's things!"

"Ow. Can we start with you not punching me?"

Molly lowered the fist she'd been pushing into Nix's bicep. She glanced at the toggle of her hoodie sheepishly.

"Sorry."

Nix held up a hand and Molly shut up. The scales on the back of Nix's thick skin were bristling to life in the same way those cactus flowers unfurled, taking in the atmosphere – air temperature, pressure, UV concentration. Or lack of. Phoenix licked the tip of one thumb and pointed it into the air. Her aquiline nose sniffed. Once, twice, and then a third time to be sure.

"Move."

She wrapped a hand around Molly's waist and half-dragged, half-marched her into a hollow in the wall banked by deactivated fuel panels. A roll of corrugated iron had caught across the lip of the alcove and Nix tugged it down. It barely reached her waist, but cover was cover.

Molly expected the thunder of the man's footsteps. She waited. She exhaled, slowly enough that her breath condensed against the iron. Silence ruled. She inhaled, tensed…

An arm darted across and pulled her further into the alcove. Her chest ached – sudden heart rate increase. Nix's breath was warm against her ear.

She said, "Your plimsolls were sticking out."

"Right. Thanks."

"*Shush.*"

A lock of her long hair brushed against Molly's cheek. Neither of them batted it away.

"All those crafts are his?"

"Can't be. Nahh… Good idea, but nah. Too different, all of them."

Then what? What could possess one man to be lordy-lording his way around a refuel station when no one else lingered? Hang about… like, who would leave a craft in a fuel station and not come back? Maybe they were all dead.

The crafts, not the people.

Hopefully.

She placed a palm against the corrugated shield and leant close to it, listening, feeling for any movement from beyond.

"He's probably gone."

"…I have a plan."

"Good. Because you've been so logical with those so far."

Phoenix glanced at her, and her eyebrows shot up her forehead. The cute smudge of ash was gone now.

Instead of sniping at Molly for her sass, Nix murmured, "I don't reckon the office will be forthcoming. Actually… scrap that. He is the office. Sorry. Should've mentioned. Uncommonly tall, male-bodied, H'katc'I Family overalls. He owns us. Alternate solution of mine, you'll remember it well… *run*. If I've got my internal topography right, and I'm pretty good with topography if I say so myself, that tower there borders the bay doors opposite death trap craft."

Did she have to call it that?

"Scale that, and it'll get us to the other side of the hangar unnoticed. You can do that."

Wasn't a question. Typical.

Between the furthest end of the hangar and the other side of the five-legged machine stood a wide support tower that probably contained whatever this moon used as generators to pump out their constant supply of Nitroxoil-tm fuel. Midway up the tower, a platform had been taken like a chunk out of the steel.

Molly eyed the platform. "Yeah."

For all Nix's bravado, when they weaved their way to the bottom of the tower and crouched behind its closest star-craft, she shot Molly a certain look and tugged on her ear. "You got this?"

"Well, bit late to be apologetic now."

"Hm."

Molly tapped her fingers along her undercut. The bristly hair comforted, reminded her – she wasn't all uselessness; she had one skill to keep up with Phoenix.

"Take this. Abseiling rope."

"*Yay.*"

Strictly speaking, it was a length of tough cabling that slithered like rubber through her hands. No use to her until she got to the ledge. Molly closed her eyes. In the darkness under her lids, peace lifted her chest. Whilst the world roared around her – a pneumatic system bubbled through a segment of wall and the moon's anti-atmosphere gale rattled titanium-plated exterior panels – her mind took the din and isolated it away from her focus.

Molly sprinted out of their hiding place. She didn't need to see the tower – only to know that it was approaching at rapid, face-smacking velocity. Human instinct did the rest.

She leapt.

Her nails scraped against the tower's panelling and the whooshing in her ears intensified. Oh god. She'd miscalculated.

Nope nope nope nope nope.

Her right hand clenched around the flattened top of a pipe.

Molly exhaled. Her lungs were burning from the need. She opened her eyes.

She dangled two metres from the ground, clenched to the only part of the wall that offered any handhold. Metal, though. The last time metal had defeated her climb, she'd been seventeen with a sprained wrist, and the metal in particular had happened to be the remains of the London Eye.

She probably would've made it, too, if the Met Police water-boat hadn't been passing and hauled her out of the Thames, a soggy delinquent.

Damn police-boat, Molly grumbled to herself as she lodged a foot into a dent barely visible in the tower. She tensed and released her shoulders, pushed her bum outwards, and shifted her weight.

Up another metre.

It took four or five repeated pulls-of-faith to get her to the ledge, despite its protrusion from the tower like a pouting lip. On the last, she overestimated. She flung herself over the ledge lip and pain spiked through her knee. Molly bit her tongue to keep from grunting aloud, but when she rolled onto her side: no blood, no metal spoke, no shard of glass. Just a heavy landing onto some steel grating.

The platform barely had space for three Mollys lying lengthways against each other. The place stank of engine oil and dust, the kind that had risen from the crafts and got up your nose and then didn't leave it until you'd sneezed more than a dozen times. Molly ran her hand across the grating.

"Oy," hissed Nix from below, "some of us are getting dead feet down here."

Patience, woman!

One end of the cabling tied to what little overhang roofed the ledge and the other draped over the edge, she closed her eyes – all the better to feel Nix's tug when it came. She stretched – *nearly – so close*. Her ankle locked around the grating. And she dragged.

Nix landed on the platform like a deer on ice.

"Don't see why you couldn't have scaled the wall yourself," Molly grumbled.

"Do I look like a lizard?"

"Do I?" she countered, raising an eyebrow pointedly.

"Yeah, yeah, my argument is invalid."

"You just don't want to admit that you need steps to reach high spaces."

"Oh shush."

Molly shut her gloating up. Not because Nix said so, but because she'd heard it, too. A tap-tap-tapping that pretended to be an innocent creaking of the pipes. At least the man chasing them had no idea who they were. If he did, he probably wouldn't've bothered sneaking towards two beings who'd gained mastery of sneaking away.

A hand settled on Molly's bicep. Nix put a finger to her lips and she jabbed her head towards the other side of the ledge not boarded by the tower wall. Yes. The sooner they got to Nix's makeshift craft and pushed off this station, the sooner they were keeping their heads intact.

Fuel shortage and craft disintegration aside.

Checking the abseiling-cable by yanking it, Molly slid herself to hang, bum out, over the ledge. The notches on the bottoms of her plimsolls caught on the grating scaling the drop.

Foot by foot, she nudged herself down the wall.

Her nose twitched. Molly winced. *Hold on.*

Her nose twitched a second time, more tickly than ever…

Molly sneezed.

Really, it was the dust's fault not hers.

"You!" a voice yelled. He angled his sonic cannon at her. "Thieves! Talk now."

"*Well…*"

"Nix… Adorable rambling won't cut it this time." Molly sighed and raised her voice. "Hi there. Look…" Her calves were stingy-ouchy from being crushed against the wall too long and she stretched herself out. No point hiding, after all. "I get it. Maybe we, I dunno, uncovered something you got going on." A fantasy. One she lived out too readily. "You can't stop us coming and going. Believe me, that's all we want to do… just go from here. Kind of need fuel for that. So s'all I ask. Fuel."

Sure, Molly had never had the gift of the gab, never been a being whose way with words got her *out* of trouble, but when the man turned and scarpered out of the hangar, she couldn't help feeling offended. She wasn't *that* bad at arguments. Really.

"Coward!" Nix yelled.

Molly nudged her shoulder against Nix's and slipped her fingertips into the woman's palm so they traced the intricate nerve-beds there disguised as decorative lines. As one, they braced the cable and shifted their weight from glute to glute as they edged down the wall. A hum resonated through the air.

"What do you reckon? We stumbled upon one man's plot to 'occupy' an entire moon-rock station?"

"Hard to tell," Nix replied, and her voice was full of conditional clauses that she didn't say – thoughts that sprinted through her big, crazy mind and offered alternate universes' worth of scenarios about one alien hiding in a fuel station. "One of those things we'll never know."

Circumstances they didn't need.

Electronic lights, dots of metallic blue that pulsed quietly from panels in the wall, decorated this corner of the hangar. Molly crossed to one. She flicked the toggle switch down. The light dot beside it dimmed into darkness. She flicked the toggle switch up. The light hummed back into existence, and the machine embedded into the wall rumbled, followed by the unmistakeable slosh of Nitroxoil-tm through the tube nozzled to the panel. Molly eyed it, the way it snaked along the floor and its other end nosed into the side of a nearby craft.

"Ooh," echoed Nix's voice.

Molly whipped around. She'd lost her again, dammit.

"A quantum transducer!" the woman squeaked from under the vehicle's engine hatch.

"You're not seriously considering… After what we just…? *God.* Besides, I don't trust anything with 'quantum' in the name. Phoenix?"

"…fine." The woman unfolded herself and was already sprinting to her craft. "But you owe me."

"One day I'm gonna teach you 'bout the necessities of a good, honest living."

"And where did that get you, waitress?"

"Shut up."

Nix chuckled. As her fingers danced across the plethora of stolen buttons in her craft, the spaceship responded, grunting to life like she'd merely reminded it that sleep was for the dead. Molly bit her lip. She'd give her best hoodie for a star-craft with headroom and corridor to gossip along. She tasted copper on her front teeth, the taste of regret. Wiping the back of her hand across her bleeding lip, she glanced at the craft she'd told Nix to stop hotwiring, with its silver body, retractable wings, and space-streamlined nose. Likely it had been modelled off the *very classic* design of a Spitfire, fifteen years ago when reminiscing about Spitfires had been in fashion. Drive-sticks and a coordination of pedals replaced touchpad navigation.

That craft probably had a separate room for beds. Those portholes lining the starboard side probably also lined a corridor… and Molly's imagination detailed a second level within the tail section that fanned out high over her head.

Now her jaw would not close. *Brilliant.*

"Not coming?" Nix interrupted.

Oh. Yeah. The masterpiece of craft-work that would kill them the moment they tried to pass through the moon's atmospheric shell. Nix would get it working. She had when she'd first built it, and, with a hunk of glistening rock at its core, she'd get it flying safe again.

Molly needed to walk past the silver craft and sit herself back in one of the two seats. The polite thing to do.

Instead, she snorted. "I'm not getting back in that death trap of a spacecraft."

"Aha!" Nix sprung out of the doorway. She pointed a finger at her, triumphant. "You want to nick one of those behemoths to fly?"

No. That was all Nix. Nix wanted to. Nix's influence…

Phoenix leaned against the window of her craft, and slipped her hands into her coat pockets. A smile danced on handsome lips. She tiptoed towards Molly, more bunny than a cat with prey. Only when she'd sidled across the distance between them did she remove her hands from her pockets. Light played off the something between her fingers.

"Not quite a gemstone, m'dear."

A screwdriver. It was a damn screwdriver, inlet with a row of gemstones that spun even the blue-light of the hangar.

Trust Nix to realise what Molly needed before she'd thought it herself.

Wrench someone else's craft open with a tool? Check. Hotwire it out of here? Check.

Molly grinned.

Raised on a diet of Tolkien, Doctor Who, and Agatha Christie, Alexandrina Brant grew up around the city of Oxford, England. After graduating from the University of Reading with joint honours in Psychology & Philosophy, she hightailed it to London to study a Master's in Linguistics at UCL, where her focus was sociolinguistics and dialect blending. She currently lives in Yorkshire with her husband and two warring cats. Her short stories have been published in several local anthologies and she is working on a steampunk novel about a linguist's journey to rescue her fiancé from phantasms and a Doctor-Who-esque sci fi about lesbian aliens trying to save a corrupt planet. She keeps up with the bookish community on Instagram @lingua_fabularum and Twitter @ caelestia_flora.

ANGEL

TONY HARRISON

The moment I saw the girl, I knew she was in danger.

My train had been delayed by almost an hour, and I spent the time listening to the thunderstorm raging outside whilst the chill half-light of the station drifted through me. I felt invisible – the sensation heightened by the indifference of the other faceless passengers, all of them as grey and soulless as their surroundings.

The girl stood no more than five metres away, her movements tense and fitful, like a startled deer preparing to flee. She was possibly eighteen or nineteen, tall and slim, dressed in a tattered denim jacket and faded jeans. Dark hair fell in waves over her shoulders; still damp from the rain, it clung to her pallid face as she stared intently at someone as yet hidden from my view. But the object of her fear did not remain out of sight for long.

The Hunter, a large, imposing shadow, gaunt and faceless, approached the girl, his features hidden beneath a wide-brimmed hat, which only served to enhance the aura of menace that surrounded him. As he took hold of the girl's arm, she struggled briefly, but when he leaned closer, speaking softly, all resistance drained from her, and she went willingly as he guided her towards the waiting train.

With a mixture of fear and excitement, I followed them. I always felt this way at the start of the hunt.

The first class carriage was gloomy, darkened by the ugly thunderheads without. The girl and her menacing custodian were the only occupants. As I entered, I could smell the faint, musty aroma of old upholstered seats embedded with decades of stale sweat.

The girl stared vacantly out of the window into the rain-soaked darkness. She did not look round as I slid the door closed, but her captor regarded me silently. Having removed his hat, his features were now revealed; his face, hard and angular; his neatly-trimmed beard and his hair – which was brushed back severely from his forehead – were completely white. He was perhaps in his mid to late fifties, though there was something in his stone-grey eyes that was much, much older.

I was immediately on my guard, certain that he could sense my trepidation, even savouring it. I sat opposite him as the train hummed into life, electricity coursing through its body like life-giving blood through veins.

"Not the best of nights to be travelling," I said with a forced casualness.

A muscle twitched almost imperceptibly just below one cold grey eye before he replied, "No, I guess not," his voice terse, his accent unmistakeably Eastern European.

His intense eyes fixed on mine and I shivered as his

voice suddenly filled my head, speaking in old Romanian. And though I did not speak the language, I understood him perfectly:

Cine ești tu?

Who are you?

"James Beaumont," I said, extending my hand.

He ignored the gesture, and I pretended not to mind, asking instead, "And you are?"

After a brief pause, he replied, "Van Myers."

I turned my attention to the girl, still gazing out of the window as though spellbound by the rain that exploded against the glass, turning to horizontal rivulets as the train picked up speed. I would have to tread carefully; I did not wish to arouse suspicion.

"And your… daughter?" I asked, feigning indifference.

Van Myers smiled, though there was no humour in it, and when he answered me, I realised that all attempts at pretence were pointless.

"Oh, she's not my daughter," he replied sardonically. "And I never had chance to ask her name. I think, perhaps, I will call her Angel. It suits her, don't you think, Mr Beaumont?"

Angel never flinched when Van Myers reached across and stroked the side of her face, but her eyes pleaded with me and, terrified as she was, she silently mouthed the words, "*Help… me…*"

Of course, she never intended for Van Myers to see this, but he missed nothing. Leaping to his feet, hissing fiercely, he struck Angel so hard her head jerked backwards, hitting the window. She did not cry out or even try to defend herself as a thin trickle of blood began to flow from the corner of her mouth.

As Van Myers raised his hand for a second blow, my vision clouded with fury and I threw myself at him.

I never reckoned on him being so fast; he spun around and grabbed me by the throat, hurling me back into my seat. Looming above me, eyes burning, feral, vicious and inhuman, he snarled, "I could tear you apart. I could devour your very soul and shatter your sanity." He released me, leaving me gasping for breath; then our eyes met, and something unspoken passed between us. He smiled, taunting, mocking and totally devoid of humour. "Perhaps I have underestimated you, Beaumont; yes, I think I have. Maybe you would prefer a challenge; a game, if you like. The girl will be the prize. Of course, if you don't think you are up to the sport..."

I tried to find within me the same lethal confidence Van Myers possessed, but the thrill of the hunt was in his eyes, and I knew he could taste my fear – yet, beneath this fear, did I not also feel the faintest tremor of anticipation?

And as I looked across at Angel – sweet, doomed Angel – I knew the choice was no longer my own.

I awoke in the empty carriage with no memory of having passed out. Only the thin silver chain on the seat beside me, a chain that had previously hung around Angel's slender neck, now twisted and distorted so that it almost resembled some ancient, crumbling ruin, told me that the game had begun, and where I was supposed to go.

The deserted cobbled streets were rivers, swollen by torrential rain. A howling wind sliced through the night, though I hardly felt the cold. Menacing storm clouds darkened the harbour where angry waves raged above the sound of the storm and I could taste the tang of salt in the air despite the driving rain.

I left the harbour and headed for the ruins of the ancient abbey high above me, silhouetted against the dark, bruised sky: a silent guardian watching over the sleeping town below, though I felt little comfort at the thought of a sentinel of cold, dead stone.

As I neared the abbey's crumbling arches, the darkness enfolded me, as chilling as a corpse's embrace, and I had the unmistakeable feeling of being watched. Not by Van Myers, of that I was certain; he would not make this game so easy.

I scanned the broken walls; seeing nothing at first, but then, as I looked upward, I saw a figure on top of a jagged column of stone almost ten metres above the rain-soaked hillside. It was only faintly darker than the night sky and unmoving, seemingly oblivious to the storm. I had almost convinced myself that I was mistaken, that the figure was, after all, nothing more than part of the misshapen stonework, when it inclined its head towards me, stretched out its arms and leapt from the pillar, disappearing into the darkness below – just as a scream cut through the storm, piercing and terrified.

I raced into the ruined interior of the abbey; that fearful cry could only have been from one person.

Van Myers was nowhere to be seen, but I saw Angel almost immediately. She was cowering against a wall, staring in terror at two cadaverous creatures as they moved sinuously around her. They seemed unaware of my presence, so, for the moment, I remained hidden.

A brief flash of lightning illuminated the scene before me, and I realised I had seen one of the figures only moments before, looking down from the top of a crumbling pillar. His spectral face was chalk-white with thin, bloodless lips and dark, hollow circles beneath his eyes. His hair was tied back in a long ponytail and his black shirt clung wetly to his sinewy arms and the prominent bones of his ribcage.

His female companion was dressed in black leather, gleaming like oil in the rain. Despite the cold night, she wore only a thin t-shirt beneath her jacket, which clung to her emaciated body, grotesquely accentuating the sunken hollow of her stomach.

Looking desperately from one creature to the other, Angel gasped in horror as the female smiled, savage and sensual, running her swollen, purple tongue over pure white fangs, hissing in anticipation.

"There is no need to fear," Ponytail said, his voice both menacing and hypnotic. "Death is a rush, and to taste it once is to desire it forever." His voice trembled feverishly as he traced a talon-like finger across Angel's face, moving slowly down, ripping her shirt, exposing soft, pale flesh.

"Oh, man!" he gasped, "what you are about to experience is the ultimate high – and it's going to last for eternity!"

I had heard enough. It was time to enter into the game.

But before I could make a move, a voice from another time spoke in my mind, a question asked in the old tongue that I again understood perfectly:

Nu vă setea?

Do you thirst?

Then a hand grabbed my shoulder and Van Myers' voice came from directly behind me.

"You disappoint me, Beaumont."

I tried to turn, but something hard smashed into the back of my head. Pain shot through me like burning quicksilver and I collapsed onto the cold, wet grass where rain pounded my body as I waited for the final blow.

It never came.

Slowly, painfully, I looked up as the ponytailed vampire spun around, howling as Van Myers leapt towards him, swinging his right arm in a slicing arc before the creature's face.

Ponytail stood, unmoving, the snarl frozen on his face as his head tilted back, blood spurting from the gaping wound in his neck. It was over in seconds as he fell at Van Myers' feet, and became dust.

Van Myers wasted no time, turning his attention to ponytail's companion who was scrabbling frantically up the vertical face of a wall like a frenzied lizard.

The blade that had effortlessly despatched the first vampire was now in Van Myers' hand, its lethal razor-sharp edge glistening in the rain. With an almost imperceptible flick of his wrist, he let it fly, just as Angel made a sudden dash for freedom.

Van Myers' aim was deadly and accurate; his victim screeched as she tumbled from the wall, hitting the ground with a thud, the blade erupting from her wasted chest only moments before she burst apart.

Her assassin did not wait to see her fall; he turned, leaping fast and high. Angel screamed as Van Myers landed before her, grabbing her hair and pulling her savagely towards him.

•

In my world, survival is not always of the fittest, but of the most cunning, for there are those – both the Vamphyrrhic and those who hunt them – that are not entirely what they seem. There are vampires who have never fully cast off the tattered remnants of their humanity and can, however misguidedly, still appear to be afflicted with human emotions.

And there are vampire hunters that are without any human emotion at all. Van Myers, it seemed, was something of both: a vampire who, so detesting his own damnable state, was impelled to hunt his own kind, though still driven by the insatiable, controlling hunger. And Angel, having served her purpose, was now his reward.

Well, as bruised and battered as I was, I was still in this game. Pushing myself agonisingly to my feet, I ran blindly, colliding with Van Myers, the momentum causing him to release Angel, pushing her aside as we fell, a tumbling mass of limbs and snapping fangs.

Then I was airborne as Van Myers hauled me roughly from the ground. Jagged stones grazed my head, digging into my back and shoulders as he pinned me against the abbey's crumbling wall, all the while, his eyes blazing hatred and murder.

"I really expected more of a fight from you," he snarled. "I should have guessed you'd be no real challenge."

My head throbbed and my vision blurred. "Sorry to disappoint you," I managed. And as the last of my strength drained away, I realised just how much I had underestimated my adversary as he threw back his head with a snarl of triumph.

Then his whole body tensed, savage victory changing to incredulity. He stumbled backwards, gazing in bewilderment at the razor-edged blade that now protruded from the centre of his chest as blood filled his mouth and seeped from his eyes like crimson tears.

Behind him, Angel reached up with bloodstained hands and pushed the blade even deeper into Van Myers' body.

Van Myers was still staring in disbelief as he slowly sank to the ground.

Then I was alone with Angel and the storm.

She runs into my arms, sobbing as I gently stroke her soft, damp hair. As she pushes her body against mine, I can feel the frantic beat of her heart. I raise her head and look deep into her eyes where fresh rain mixes with salt tears.

Does she understand? Does it matter to her that the choice was not my own? Does she even care that I hunger too?

She moves her head to one side, exposing the smooth, soft flesh of her neck. She does this without instruction, in silent acceptance of her fate, as I lower my head and claim my prize.

•

Previously employed as an armed police officer in the MOD, then as a live music/karaoke entertainer in Spain, Tony Harrison now works as a full-time admin assistant and part-time writer, reading and writing horror, sci-fi and fantasy.

During the 90s he had several Gothic horror stories and some depressing poems published in a Goth fanzine called Pink Flamingo (no, he doesn't know, either!). More recently, the ghost stories 'Daddy's home' and '42' have appeared in the anthologies, In The Dark and Inkerman Street; the epic comedy poem 'Legend of Sam Sasquatch' in Picture This, and in 2018, the ghost story 'Resurrection Act' appeared in the Crossing The Tees anthology. His first story in Harvey Duckman was in Volume 5. He has been spending the 2020 lockdown working on a fantasy/steampunk novel with his twelve-year-old nephew.

A VERY HAPPY MONDAY

D.T. LANGDALE

Uno had never been more excited to wear Kevin. Even before his alarm began playing BBC Radio 2, Uno was out of bed, his tentacles quivering. He crossed the bedroom to his wardrobe chiller and opened it, stepping back as a cloud of cold air hissed past him. The DJ was discussing last night's *Love Island* and Uno made a mental note to remember the details. Kevin had been a big fan, after all.

He selected Kevin's skin from the ice-cold chamber and squeezed himself through the back flap, pushing his tentacles right to the toes. As the last of his suckers attached, Uno headed for the shower to hose it down, unable to stop smiling.

'Step On' by the Happy Mondays came on the radio. And what a Monday it would be. Uno clapped Kevin's hands together. On any normal day, Kevin would wear a polo shirt and jeans. But, this was no ordinary day. Uno slipped on a pressed blue shirt and tucked it into crisp chinos. He slicked back his head hair and chest hair, before doing up his buttons right to the collar.

Today, all his hours of overtime would be rewarded. He knew Kevin had been the right choice. Finally, with a 'senior' title, he would be accepted as a true member of the Brood. Mother would be so proud. He even had his celebration planned – a platter of raw meat, slathered in ice cream, with *You've Got Mail* on repeat. Humming brightly, he made himself a coffee in a bamboo travel mug, packed his smashed avocado sandwiches (which he always threw away) into his leather satchel, popped in his headphones and headed out to work.

•

Uno rode the 8.05am to Leeds, listening to the radio all the way to the office, noting down possible conversation points. When he reached his desk, he poured his coffee into Kevin's wilting desk plant and arranged all the stationery so it aligned to his keyboard, as Kevin would have. That was when he noticed Ben in his manager's office. He was wearing a light blue shirt and chinos too. *Well played, Ben.*

"Did you see *Love Island* last night, Kev?" Sally, his colleague, asked, peering over her desk divider. But Uno's attention was fixed on his manager's office. Sally followed his gaze, turning with one knee on her swivel chair. "Oh, it's today, isn't it? Look, Ben's only been here a couple of months. There's no way they'd make him Senior Account Manager."

Uno wanted to believe her. But he'd seen his manager's

flirting face before. The way she twirled the end of her ponytail, the strange tongue flicking. Ben was talking with confidence, his muscles in a state of permanent tension. Even his buttocks were taut. Uno wasn't sure if Kevin's could do that. He noted all this down, wondering if this is what it felt like to be on *Love Island*.

Ben stepped out, all grins. His manager beckoned Uno over, her face severe. All four of Uno's hearts sank and Kevin's legs felt heavy. Ben winked as he passed and Uno made a note of this too. He really had set his hopes on Kevin.

Oh, well, he thought. He would have to put celebrations on hold. Because if Kevin couldn't have the promotion, Uno would have Ben.

•

Humans really were fascinating creatures. No matter the events of the day, they would find solace in routine. Uno pondered this as he watched Ben through his kitchen window, fresh from his promotion, mixing a protein drink and boiling half a dozen eggs. He'd be leaving for the gym any minute. No hint of celebration. Uno had struggled to process this behaviour at first. But, hidden inside the rhododendron bush behind Ben's Kirkstall Lane flat share, Uno finally understood. Routine was their anchor.

He thought back through his other skins and the notes he'd made for them. Each was tied to a habit. Whether it was a morning coffee, an evening glass of red, or a second pass by the office biscuit plate. Uno had always been careful to note these details without realising their significance. They were the key to a successful assimilation. Even colleagues would notice their absence. If Sally stopped adding four spoons of sugar to her coffee, there'd be uproar. She'd have to field questions about the diet she was on and why the sudden change in her life's direction.

Humans are attuned to routine. To habit. They need it. And Ben was no different. He'd swiped Kevin's promotion from under his nose. Kevin's overtime no match for Ben's twitching buttocks. Yet, here he was. The newly appointed Senior Account Manager just going about his routine.

Uno was still revelling in the revelation long after he'd pulled Ben into the bush, paralysed his muscles with his venom tipped stinger and slurped out his insides. He couldn't wait to call Mother and tell her all about it. Especially his new promotion.

Taking care not to crease him, Uno packed Ben away into his work satchel and scampered back to Leeds station just in time for the 7.15pm back to Saltaire.

•

Uno's mother wasn't happy. Not happy at all. Uno had been curled up on the sofa when the headlights of her black Range Rover washed through his window. He'd paused *You've Got Mail,* unfurled his tentacles from around the leather cushion and put his platter of raw meat slathered in ice cream on the coffee table. He'd been excited to see her, to tell her his news, but the moment he saw her face, he knew he'd messed up.

Bodyguards flanked the door, staring out at his street, arms folded. His brother and sister. They didn't even say hello. Mother strode in and removed an earpiece, letting the coiled plastic dangle down over her shoulder. Her human suit had the wrinkles of age, with lean muscles, sharp eyes and hands that could strangle a bull. Her suit was also the head of the United Kingdom's Secret Intelligence Service (SIS).

She pushed past, led him through his own kitchen to the living room, turned and rested her hands on her hips.

"I got my promotion!" Uno stretched his suckers into a wide smile.

"What *were* you thinking, Uno?"

"I… I…"

"Bring down your suits. Both of them."

"But, Mother."

Mother pursed her lips. There was no arguing. He slithered upstairs, chuntering under his breath. He retrieved Ben and Kevin from the chilled wardrobe and laid them side-by-side on the dining room table, their faces pointing blankly to the ceiling.

"Do you see the problem here, Uno?"

Uno glanced from Ben to Kevin.

Mother's eyes narrowed. "They work together," she said. And, when Uno didn't respond. "In the same office."

Still, Uno stared at his suits.

Her eyes narrowed further still.

"How will you explain Kevin's absence while you're enjoying Ben's new promotion?"

Realisation dawned. Acid rolled around his stomachs. Shame stabbed at his skin. He felt his body slump, oozing into the ground.

"I messed up," he said.

"Yes, Uno, you did."

He groaned. "I'll never be a full member of the Brood."

He imagined his brother and sister whispering outside.

"Let's face it," she said. "Senior Account Manager was hardly chasing the stars. You're meant for more than that."

Uno sank further into the ground.

"You know why we do this, right, Uno?" Her voice was soft.

Uno had the answer memorised. "Of course. IAE: infiltrate, assimilate, energise."

"Well, yes, that's the official line." She ran a hand through her grey bob and dropped onto a dining chair. "Come, sit down."

Uno slithered to a chair, hoisted himself up.

"We've been doing the whole IAE routine for millennia. Assimilating planets, races, species; feeding, energising, moving on. The same routine. It's how we survive. Though, I'm not sure how much longer we can keep going."

She searched his face.

"You see, we might be surviving, but we're not living.

On Earth, they live. Discos, roller blades, jogging. We've never known anything like it. But, I think you do."

"I don't understand, Mother."

"What were you doing before I walked in?"

Uno suddenly didn't want to meet her eyes. He was sure she wouldn't approve. "I was watching a film. *You've Got Mail*."

"And why, Uno, were you watching that?"

Uno thought for a moment. "Because it makes me feel…"

"Yes?"

"Soggy."

Mother lowered her voice, leaning forward. "You know what I like?"

Uno shook his tentacles.

"Eating bacon-wrapped Twiglets while listening to the Spice Girls. In the bath. I can't even tell you how I discovered it. But, that feeling. That wonderful, soggy feeling. No other Brood member understands."

Uno thought back to his realisation outside Ben's kitchen window. The fascinating ability of humans to take pleasure in the most mundane of activities. Was this what Mother meant?

"So, I'm not in trouble?"

"Far from it, Uno. I have a job for you."

She clicked her fingers and the bodyguards strode in, picked up Ben and strode out. They didn't even say goodbye.

"They'll assume Ben's role at the agency."

"How wi–"

"I'll give them all your notes, don't worry. They'll blend in."

"What should I do?"

"I want you to think of the person that makes you the soggiest."

Easy question, Uno thought. "Tom Hanks."

"Alright." Mother clapped her hands together. "Uno, I want you to assimilate Tom Hanks."

Uno stared. He felt his breath quicken, even at the dizzy prospect. His imagination began to work in overdrive. He spoke very slowly, expecting he'd misheard her.

"I need to assimilate Tom Hanks. And, if I do, I'll be a full member of the Brood?"

Surely not.

"You won't just be a full member, Uno. You'll be our saviour."

"How?"

"You'll free us. You'll teach us how to *live*."

•

Uno lay in bed, feeling the soft duvet on his flesh, playing the day back. A bird sang outside, quickly drowned out by a passing ambulance. He couldn't even begin to plan the days ahead. His routine as Kevin had been so constant, it felt very strange knowing he wouldn't need to catch up on *Love Island*. Well, maybe he could catch up a little.

As he rolled over and closed all of his eyes, another

feeling tumbled over in his stomach. It felt bouncy. Like hundreds of feet jumping up and down inside him. He knew exactly what it was.

Uno couldn't wait to wear Tom Hanks.

•

D.T. Langdale is a professional copywriter and author with a passion for quirky sci-fi and fantasy. He has had short stories published in Phantasmagoria magazine and the Cozy Villages of Death anthology, as well as flash fiction published in the Museum of Walking's Winter Chill anthology, Tritely Challenged: Volume 2 and Adverbially Challenged: Volume 5. When not writing, he's often found walking the Yorkshire countryside with his fiancé, listening out for lapwings. He is a member of the British Fantasy Society and Clockhouse and Northwrite writing groups. Find out more about D.T. Langdale on Twitter @dtlangdale.

Also available from Sixth Element Publishing
in paperback and eBook:

Harvey Duckman Presents… Volume 1
Published April 2019
*including stories by: Kate Baucherel,
D.W. Blair, A.L. Buxton, R. Bruce Connelly,
Joseph Carrabis, Nate Connor, Marios Eracleous,
Craig Hallam, C.G. Hatton, Mark Hayes,
Peter James Martin, Reino Tarihmen, J.L. Walton,
Graeme Wilkinson and Amy Wilson.*

www.6epublishing.net

Also available from Sixth Element Publishing
in paperback and eBook:

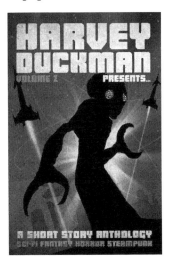

Harvey Duckman Presents… Volume 2
Published October 2019
including stories by: Peter James Martin, Ben McQueeney,
A.L. Buxton, R. Bruce Connelly, Phoebe Darqueling,
Melissa Wuidart Phillips, Marios Eracleous, Nate
Connor, James Porter, Joseph Carrabis, Cheryllynn Dyess,
Erudessa Gentian, Liz Tuckwell, JL Walton and Amy Wilson,
as well as a bonus 'Harvey Duckman' story by Mark Hayes,
and a foreword by Craig Hallam.

www.6epublishing.net

Also available from Sixth Element Publishing
in paperback and eBook:

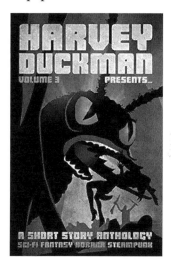

Harvey Duckman Presents… Volume 3
Published October 2019
*including stories by: Peter James Martin, Ben McQueeney,
A.L. Buxton, R. Bruce Connelly, Phoebe Darqueling,
Melissa Wuidart Phillips, Marios Eracleous, Nate
Connor, James Porter, Joseph Carrabis, Cheryllynn Dyess,
Erudessa Gentian, Liz Tuckwell, JL Walton and Amy Wilson,
as well as a bonus 'Harvey Duckman' story by Mark Hayes,
and a foreword by Craig Hallam.*

www.6epublishing.net

Also available from Sixth Element Publishing
in paperback and eBook:

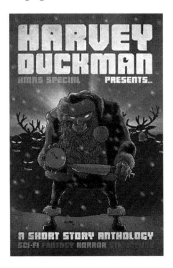

Harvey Duckman Presents…
Christmas Special 2019
Published December 2019
including stories by: Thomas Gregory, Andy Hill,
Peter James Martin, Craig Hallam, Kate Baucherel,
Cheryllynn Dyess, Marios Eracleous, Zack Brooks,
Ben McQueeney, Maggie Kraus, Gerald Wiley,
Lynne Lumsden Green, Mark Hayes,
Ben Sawyer and R. Bruce Connelly.

www.6epublishing.net

Also available from Sixth Element Publishing
in paperback and eBook:

Harvey Duckman Presents… Volume 4
Published March 2020
*including stories by: Adrian Bagley, Crysta K Coburn,
Thomas Gregory, Christine King, Peter James Martin,
John Holmes-Carrington, A.L. Buxton, Zack Brooks,
Fred Johnson, Ben McQueeney, Keld Hope, Deborah
Barwick, Jon Hartless, R. Bruce Connelly, and Mark Hayes,
as well as a bonus 'Harvey Duckman' story by Andy Hill,
and a foreword by Amy Wilson.*

www.6epublishing.net

Also available from Sixth Element Publishing
in paperback and eBook:

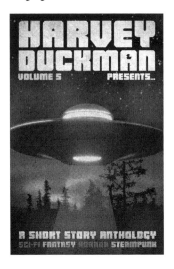

Harvey Duckman Presents… Volume 5
Published July 2020
*including stories by: Adrian Bagley, Kate Baucherel,
A.L. Buxton, Aidan Cairnie, Joseph Carrabis,
R. Bruce Connelly, Tony Harrison, Mark Hayes,
Scott Howard, Peter James Martin, Alex Minns,
Andrew Openshaw, Melissa Rose Rogers, Kathrine
Machon and Liz Tuckwell, with a foreword from
fantasy author Ben McQueeney.*

www.6epublishing.net

Also available from Sixth Element Publishing
in paperback and eBook:

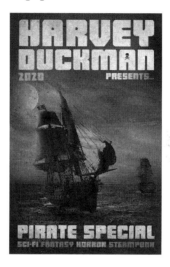

Harvey Duckman Presents… Pirate Special 2020
Published September 2020
includes stories by: Amy Wilson, Ben Sawyer,
Kate Baucherel, Mark Hayes, Melissa Wuidart
Phillips, C.G. Hatton, A.L. Buxton, Reino Tarihmen,
Liz Tuckwell, R. Bruce Connelly, Mark Sayeh,
Christine King, Joseph Carrabis, Loïc Baucherel,
Nils Nisse Visser, Peter James Martin and Andy Hill.

www.6epublishing.net

Find Harvey on Facebook:
www.facebook.com/harveyduckman

Find Harvey on Twitter:
twitter.com/DuckmanHarvey

Harvey Duckman Presents… is edited by C.G. Hatton

C.G. Hatton is the author of the fast-paced, military science fiction books set in the high-tech Thieves' Guild universe of galactic war and knife-edge intrigue. She has a PhD in geology and a background in journalism, and is currently working on the ninth book in the Thieves' Guild series, as well as compiling and editing more volumes of Harvey Duckman Presents…

Find out more at www.cghatton.com

•

www.harveyduckman.com

Printed in Great Britain
by Amazon